We gratefully acknowledge the support of the Canada Council for the Arts and the Ontario Arts Council for our publishing program. We also acknowledge the financial support of the Government of Canada.

Cover design: Val Fullard

Good Girls is a work of fiction. All the characters and situations portrayed in this book are fictitious and any resemblance to persons living or dead is purely coincidental.

Library and Archives Canada Cataloguing in Publication

Fardin, Shalta Dicaire, 1986-, author
    Good girls / Shalta Dicaire Fardin and Sarah Sahagian.

(Inanna young feminist series)
Issued in print and electronic formats.
ISBN 978-1-77133-345-0 (paperback).-- ISBN 978-1-77133-346-7 (epub). --
ISBN 978-1-77133-347-4 (kindle).-- ISBN 978-1-77133-348-1 (pdf)

    I. Sahagian, Sarah, 1986-, author II. Title.

PS8611.A7464G66 2016   C813'.6   C2016-904855-1
                                               C2016-904856-X

Printed and bound in Canada

Inanna Publications and Education Inc.
210 Founders College, York University
4700 Keele Street, Toronto, Ontario M3J 1P3 Canada
Telephone: (416) 736-5356   Fax (416) 736-5765
Email: inanna.publications@inanna.ca
Website: www.inanna.ca

FSC
www.fsc.org
MIX
Paper from
responsible sources
FSC® C004071

GOOD GIRLS

a novel by

SHALTA DICAIRE FARDIN
and SARAH SAHAGIAN

◑INANNA
Young Feminist Series

For my ABC, Elmwood.
        —Shalta Dicaire Fardin

For my students.
Always remember that you are strong,
capable, professional women.
        —Sarah Sahagian

CONTENTS

1.

OCTAVIA

BY ALL ACCOUNTS, the gathering had turned to total mayhem. It was supposed to be a small party for twenty select people at Octavia's country house. Octavia had planned the list with great precision, taking care to invite a mix of friends from school and from the lake, omitting those who didn't fit her vision for the perfect weekend. It was the very end of summer, and she wanted to make it a party her closest friends would never forget. Every moment would be Instagram-worthy, Octavia thought, while giddily picturing the disappointed faces of those only permitted to attend through the window of Instagram uploads and Snapchats. No one was supposed to get arrested though.

The music was already blaring when a group of girls screamed, "Turn it up!" Their hands were in the air as they hoisted one of their friends onto the dining room table, her heels scuffing the immaculate varnish. Octavia sat in the corner, nursing a drink, pretending to pay attention to the conversation around her. She was, in fact, deep in thought.

Sophomore year of high school was about to begin, with Octavia's life unfolding just the way she wanted it to. Intention was important to Octavia. She was a bit of an enigma to her peers. She had always exercised a great amount of control in life; however, she was simultaneously relaxed about a great deal – especially school. This unusual mix of characteristics was likely the result of the improbable match of her (no longer together) parents. Octavia thought of them: her father was so exact and strident; her mother, gentle and soft-spoken, a total hippie.

The party swirled around Octavia as her mind slowly focused back on her surroundings. The alcohol was taking effect. She remembered the last vodka shot she did with her friend Ella. Octavia giggled to herself over how, despite being sixteen, a full year older than Octavia, Ella had spit out the alcohol in disgust. Ella clearly was not a connoisseur of hard liquor.

Octavia turned to face the large bay window at the other side of the room. She could see Molly, one of her best friends, talking to a strange man with a rower's body. He looked older, maybe around twenty-five. They were laughing about something or other, as he leaned in closer and whispered in Molly's ear. "How did he get here?" Octavia thought to herself, suddenly suspicious of this mature-looking man with broad shoulders. She'd never seen him before, so he wasn't on the official guest list. Slowly Octavia scanned the living room and realized there were at least forty people there. To make matters worse, there were countless others in the backyard.

Octavia could feel trouble brewing. Knots in her stomach signaled this event was about to get completely and utterly out of control. Her mind wandered to Marcus. If she could find him, Octavia believed he would make this mayhem right.

Octavia left the house to look for him and quickly made her way down to the lower deck. Her boyfriend Marcus was seated with his friends at her stepmother's prized outdoor dining area. Everyone assembled seem to be dressed in varying patterns of plaid. They were smoking joints they rolled themselves, relaxed and oblivious to the surrounding chaos.

Marcus caught Octavia's eye as she walked down the stairs. She gave him her best sultry smile, making sure not to betray the butterflies in her stomach. The truth was that every look from him still made her heart jump. She couldn't believe he was hers.

Marcus and Octavia's families had been friends since they were children, and Octavia had been in love with Marcus from the first second she saw him. It was difficult for any girl who met him not to fall for Marcus, with his chiseled good looks and confidence. Marcus was gorgeous. He wasn't simply handsome, however. He also had a certain *je ne sais quoi*. He was *cool*. That was the only way to describe him. His knowledge of music was encyclopedic. He liked the best bands long before anyone else even knew they existed, and his kissing abilities were legendary amongst the women of Montreal.

Growing up, Marcus had thought of Octavia as a nuisance, a little girl he was forced to entertain when their families got together. Octavia had worried she would be doomed to pine for Marcus for the rest of her life. She had even considered writing soppy poetry about her unrequited love. For years, the four-year age difference between Marcus and Octavia seemed like a gulf that could never be bridged, but something happened earlier that very summer that had changed things, maybe forever.

That July, when Marcus saw Octavia walking down the street to her house in her tight white tennis dress, he had done a double take from his car. Octavia thought about that moment often. She had just come from a tennis match, and was talking on her phone when Marcus drove right up to her, and declared, "Well, look at you." At that moment, Octavia knew Marcus was ready to see her as more than a little girl, and she was on the cusp of achieving her heart's desire. That moment was two months ago now, and the pair had been inseparable ever since.

When Marcus saw his girlfriend approach through the partying crowd of inebriated people, he called out to her. "Hey, come here, Tavi." This was his affectionate nickname for her. He pulled her down onto his lap, then passed the joint he was smoking to his friend. Octavia leaned her mouth in for a kiss.

Suddenly, an unwelcome voice ruined the intimate moment Octavia had been craving all night. "Bro, can we get this party started? Let's be real, this kind of blows," said Connor with a grunt. He looked disheveled, with a noticeable red stain on his shirt that had not been there earlier in the evening. Connor was one of Marcus' oldest friends, and also happened to be one of Octavia's least favourite people.

Octavia sat up briskly, "What do you have in mind then?" she asked and made a show of rolling her eyes in his direction.

Connor mimicked her. She hated him. He was a trust fund loser. She was used to kids with mommy and daddy issues, but he was a special breed. He had lost his heiress mother as a child, and with his absent father living with a supermodel in Berlin, Connor had become an incredible brat. He was technically enrolled at McGill University, but barely went to school. He was always the first to take a perfectly good party and turn it into something more ... destructive. Tonight would be no different. His friends only tolerated him because his brashness was fun and, to put it bluntly, they felt bad for him.

Connor got up and announced that it was time to leave, shooting Marcus a determined look. Marcus still had his arm around Octavia, and though she looked at her boyfriend pleadingly, it was clear he was going to follow his friend. As the guys got up to leave, Connor sneered at her. "Bros over hoes, girl."

Octavia hated statements like that. She was often in the presence of boys, and heard them saying disgusting things about girls she knew when they thought she wasn't paying attention. She wasn't the type of girl to let anyone point a statement like that in her direction though. "You're a douche bag," she hissed.

Despite her altercation with Connor, Octavia still walked her boyfriend out to the garage. She hated his friends, but all the hatred in the world couldn't snuff out her undeniable urge to be close to Marcus for as long as possible. The goodbye itself, however, was markedly unsatisfying. Marcus left Octavia with a lukewarm kiss on her cheek, her throat burning while she tried to hold back tears.

Marcus and his friends piled into his black Range Rover, while Octavia watched the white headlights cut through the dark, stinging her eyes. She stood outside and watched the car get smaller and smaller, until it reached the edge of her family's private driveway and she could no longer see the headlights in the distance. Now she was just mad. Part of her had thought Marcus wouldn't actually leave. She had thought he might change his mind at the last minute, or at least ask her to join them.

Octavia felt the anger welling inside her, mixed with embarrassment. It was a lethal cocktail.

The rabbi was getting up to give a speech when Mordecai D. Schwartz's cell phone rang loudly and clearly. Embarrassed, he turned the ringer on silent and stepped into the hall to take the call.

Upon his return to the banquet hall, his wife looked over at him furiously, "What was that about? You can't just get up and walk out of my nephew's Bar Mitzvah, Morty," Shira complained.

"I know, but I have to go right away," replied an anxious Mordecai. He could barely get the words out fast enough. "That was Lisa Roberston. She told me their country house has been broken into and vandalized. The police think it was some kids who were at a party, at our house. The Robertsons think Octavia invited them up." He hadn't paused for a single breath as he relayed the events to Shira. She, his wife of fourteen years, took it all in with wide eyes and an open mouth.

Shira was shrill at this point, but Mordecai thought only of his daughter. Octavia having a party at their summer home, without their permission? It was the unthinkable, the last straw he might have seen coming but was not ready to confront. Mordecai considered calling Octavia's mother, but thought better. He hadn't spoken to Sophie in any form but email for two years, and he rather preferred it that way. Mordecai knew that Sophie had never truly forgiven him for walking out on her when she was pregnant, breaking off their engagement simply because his parents found her bohemian nature objectionable. He had not forgiven himself either, and yet, he had never actually apologized to Sophie. He had not managed to get out the words, "I'm sorry." Every time he spoke to Sophie, whether she evoked longing, nostalgia, or blinding rage over her lax parenting style, Mordecai always felt too much. He disliked this because feelings made him profoundly uncomfortable.

"You cannot go. The rabbi is speaking, and we haven't done the hora." Shira was grasping at whatever she could to keep her husband from leaving. She hated Octavia. She tried to hide it, and Mordecai tried his best not to notice it, but it was clear she had nothing but disdain for her stepdaughter, and for her stepdaughter's mother.

This time, Shira's attempts at manipulation did not work. "Put another zero on the cheque," Mordecai instructed. "I'm sorry, I have to go right away." He kissed her forehead and headed for the door.

It was morning by the time Mordecai's driver pulled up to his home in the Laurentians. The lake was quiet and calm. Mordecai was relieved to see his home stood in one piece, and for a moment, he thought maybe there had been a mistake, that Octavia hadn't thrown a party at all. There were only two cars in the driveway, perhaps Octavia had one friend up and the Robertsons had completely overreacted, (like they did when Mordecai installed a water feature over the lake the year before), he thought.

Walking up the stairs to the front door, his fantasy of it all being a mistake was quickly erased, as he was met with a motley collection of beer cans, red plastic cups, and designer suede boots. As he crossed the threshold of his home and closed the door behind him, his anger became volcanic.

Mordecai made his way through the house, simmering. When

he finally entered Octavia's bedroom without knocking, his anger erupted. He was met with the sight of his daughter, in bed, with a guy. Upon seeing her father, Octavia, shot up in bed. She was horrified as she met his gaze. "What is the meaning of this, Octavia?" he demanded, watching his daughter intently, her mascara smeared across her eyes. She said nothing.

The boy next to Octavia woke, and quickly realized what was happening. "And who are you?" Mordecai screamed.

"I'm gay! And I'm going," replied Octavia's friend David. He grabbed his pants and left the room, giving Octavia a plaintive look.

Octavia hugged her knees and whispered a barely audible, "Hi, Daddy."

Mordecai practically growled. "You have no idea how hard it was for me to get here, Octavia. I had to *drive* here. I *drove* here," he emphasized. "You know, *on the ground*. I don't do 'the ground,' Octavia." This was true. Mordecai usually flew the company jet everywhere, but it had been too foggy in Toronto for the jet to takeoff, so he was stuck driving his Maybach the entire way. It was a true top one percent of first world problems.

Octavia remained silent. She was still fixated on Marcus. Was this the end? Was he over her? Why wasn't he here to help her deal with this sticky situation? Her father was talking in an endless stream, but she only heard snippets. She felt tired and defeated. When her father told her about the vandalized house next door, she felt awful thinking of Lisa Roberston's endless cream walls and crisp linen sofas, which her father informed her were now covered in a sticky combination of egg and red spray paint. Octavia knew, of course, who the vandal had been. It was definitely Connor. Octavia remembered the red stain on his shirt, just like the red spray paint her father was now murmuring about being all over the Robertsons' walls. Connor had probably done it in-between smoking joints. Octavia knew he always travelled with his spray paint, ready either to defile public property or people's homes, depending on his mood.

Octavia wondered if she told her father the truth, would Marcus never speak to her again out of loyalty to Connor and his posse of delinquents?

She looked back at her father but tried to avoid eye contact. Her head was pounding and she felt close to throwing up. She knew what he would ask: "Octavia, do you know who did this?"

And when he did, she made no reply. He continued, "This isn't going to go away. The police need to know. This is serious."

Octavia tried to talk but it came out as a squeak instead. Her lip quivered and she wrung her hands nervously. As Octavia started to cry, her father sat down on the bed next to her. He let his daughter sob as he pulled her into his arms.

"I know you didn't do it. I know you would never destroy someone else's property, but you shouldn't be socializing with people who would do such a thing, either. This is it, sweetheart. We are done with this phase."

"Okay, okay, I'm done!" she cried in response.

"You have no idea," replied her father in a stern but gentle tone. Octavia knew she was defeated. No matter what it cost her, she had to give up the extremely inconvenient truth. So she named the names, leaving it until the end to explain Connor and his cronies were friends Marcus had brought. Her father sighed in disappointment as he pulled out his phone to dial the local police.

Octavia stared out at the lake through the open window, bleary eyed.

When he was finally done speaking with the authorities, Mordecai turned to Octavia. His daughter's dark curly tendrils and piercing brown eyes were strikingly beautiful, despite the smudged makeup and bed head. He wondered if he and Octavia's mother had just taken better care of their daughter, would something like this have happened?

"I'm going to call your mother," announced Mordecai. The words made Octavia's stomach drop to the floor. No matter how badly she misbehaved, her parents had never teamed up against her before. Octavia had no idea what would happen, but she had a strong suspicion it would change her whole life.

2.

ALLIE

"I AM SO EXCITED for school to start!" Allie Denning said out loud. Allie made sure she only talked to herself like this in the privacy of her own room because it was a habit her mother disliked. Even though she knew most people would think it made her appear unstable, Allie could not help wanting to have conversations with herself sometimes, mostly because she was certain no one really understood her feelings but her.

Allie had friends, and plenty of them. Since kindergarten, Allie had attended Boston's most elite all-girls prep school, Anne Bradstreet College, affectionately known as ABC by its students. Having always attended the same school, Allie had been close with the same group of girls since she was five years old. Now that they were in the tenth grade, they were considered the "good girls" of ABC. They were girls who never cheated on a test (Who needs to cheat when you stayed up until one a.m. studying the night before?), never touched pot (It just takes time away from doing homework!), and didn't bother staying out past curfew (Why get into a fight with your parents?). Most of all, however, Allie and her girlfriends were defined by the fact that they all wanted to go to Ivy League schools, and they would do whatever it took to get there.

Today, Allie was overjoyed to be going to Anne Bradstreet College's uniform shop, where she would pick up her new skirt, blouse, and blazer. Even though it was the same uniform

Allie had been wearing most of her life, it was still exciting to go to the shop each year. It signalled a new start. Allie hated summers, the time when she was away from the academic and extra-curricular rigour of ABC. She had spent all of July and August craving the start of classes, and now, the beginning of school was finally in sight. In only a few days, school would be in full swing!

Unfortunately, Allie's reverie was soon interrupted. "Hurry up!" Called her mother in a brisk tone from downstairs.

Allie doubled her speed, grabbing an elastic to force her thick, wavy brown tendrils into a neat ponytail. She surveyed herself in the mirror to make sure she appeared put-together. Allie did not care that much about whether or not people found her attractive (beauty is subjective, after all) but she did want people to think she looked polished.

Allie Denning was always a picture of preppy good taste, and today was no different. She wore an a-line floral Lilly Pulitzer dress with a simple white cardigan from J.Crew. Around her neck, Allie donned her most treasured possession, the string of pearls her Grandma Trudy had given her for her twelfth birthday. As Allie's grandmother was fond of saying, "No outfit is complete without a string of pearls!"

Satisfied with her appearance, Allie rushed downstairs to the kitchen where her mother was waiting. She knew her mom was roughly thirty seconds away from screaming at her louder than a Fox News anchor interviewing a democrat. This was ironic, as Sybilla had actually volunteered to campaign for Senator Elizabeth Warren.

"You're late," reproached Sybilla sternly.

"I know, Mom. I'm sorry. I lost track of time reading *Pride and Prejudice,* and before I knew it, it was eight a.m. and I wasn't even dressed."

"Allie, why do you have to read so many books about rich white people with bourgeois problems?"

"Mom, *Pride and Prejudice* is a classic story of love, betrayal, and the problems with judging people based on first impressions. It's not just a story about women who go to fancy balls all the time," Allie protested.

"I really wish you would read that copy of *The Handmaid's Tale* I got you. Some feminist literature would do you good." Sybilla grabbed her car keys off the kitchen island. "And please, don't go on that rant again about how Jane Austen is feminist literature. I have no interest in hearing your fledgling adolescent theories. I have a hard enough time enduring the essays my undergraduate students write at Wellesley." With that, Sybilla and Allie headed for the garage and piled into the family's forest green BMW SUV.

As they drove the familiar route from their ivy-covered home in Cambridge to ABC's Mission Hill campus, Allie couldn't help but smile. She knew that in no time at all, she would be back to being top of her class in English, history and French, and to winning debate tournaments like there was no tomorrow. Anne Bradstreet College was Allie's element. It was what she lived for.

Unfortunately for Allie, Sybilla did not share Allie's enthusiasm about ABC. "Why are you grinning like a Cheshire cat?" remarked Sybilla as she navigated the streets of Cambridge, passing through the imposing brick buildings of Harvard's campus.

"I'm not, Mom. I'm just ... happy," said Allie.

"Happy about what? Are you seriously this enthused about picking up your uniform? It's the same outfit you've worn every school day for the past eleven years, just a few inches longer to accommodate that growth spurt you had this spring. When it comes down to it, you are getting excited for an extremely overpriced polyester skirt."

Allie stayed silent, hoping her mother would end her rant if she did not contradict her. Sybilla, however, had more to say. "It costs about $1500 each year to get you a new uniform that fits. I used to think school uniforms would save parents money." She paused for a brief guffaw. "Well, that was until I had a daughter who went to ABC. For the money it costs to buy one uniform at this school of yours, I could have clothed an entire high school of children in Malawi."

Allie hated these tirades of her mother's. Sybilla was willing to drive Allie to ABC, but Allie always had to sit through a twenty-minute speech about how wasteful and unnecessary it was for her to be a student there.

"Sometimes I wish I had never let your father and grandmother convince me to send you kids to private schools. I went to an inner-city public school back in Detroit, and I went on to receive a PhD in economics..." Sybilla trailed off, lost for a moment in her past life.

"Mom, ABC is an excellent academic institution. I'm glad I go there. I think it's a great education that will really help me in the future." Allie said this in a firm tone, even though she knew it was a mistake to have said anything at all.

"Oh, Allie, it's an environment that babies you. ABC brags about how none of their classes ever have more than twenty girls in them, so that teachers can give each student *individual attention,*" Sybilla said, making a face. "All that does is prevent you from becoming an independent learner."

Allie didn't believe this was true. She did feel challenged at ABC, especially on the debate team. She *was* becoming an independent thinker. So independent, in fact, that she barely agreed with a single word her own mother said anymore.

Allie closed her hazel eyes and wondered if it was possible for her mother ever to be satisfied with her? She was one of the highest-achieving young women most people had ever met. Not only that, but she never got into any inappropriate shenanigans involving sex, alcohol, or drugs. As "good" a girl as Allie was, there simply did not seem to be a way for Sybilla to think Allie was good enough.

Sybilla had grown up with nothing and had earned everything for herself. Her parents were Lebanese Christians who had emigrated from Beirut. When the young Sybilla arrived in America at the age of five, she did not speak a word of English. Her family had so little money they were forced to live in one of the roughest neighbourhoods in Detroit (with the kind of schools where disenfranchised youth brought knives to class). Sybilla's high school could not even afford textbooks for every student, and yet Sybilla had managed to earn a full scholarship to Columbia. At Columbia, Sybilla was at the top of her class in no time, completing an undergraduate degree in economics before earning her PhD from Harvard in record time.

Sybilla was self-made, but no matter how hard Allie worked, it could never be said that she had pulled herself up by her bootstraps. With two parents who were Harvard legacies and a great-grandfather who was president of that university in the 1950s, Allie Denning had Harvard College in her blood. Even though she was a hard-working girl who received near perfect grades, volunteered at soup kitchens, and was the first tenth grader in ABC history to make captain of the debate team, none of this made Allie any less privileged. It simply meant she took advantage of the opportunities her privilege afforded her.

Nonetheless, Allie was determined to make every aspect of tenth grade go smoothly, but there was just one problem. His name was Jack Mansbridge, and he was her new debate coach.

Jack, a first-year political science student at Harvard, had only graduated from ABC's brother school, Hillsview College, the year before. Just that past spring, Jack and Allie's older brother Aram won the American National Debate Championships. Of course, Allie knew it was impressive, but she still was not sure if she trusted Jack as a coach. After all, he was the guy she had gotten in water gun fights with at her family's house in Martha's Vineyard only a month before.

Jack was a regular guest of Aram's at the beach house every summer, and he always teased Allie mercilessly whenever he was there. Jack referred to Allie as "The Princess of the Prudes," because she was very vocal about her distaste for the sorts of bathing suits that leave half a girl's bottom exposed to the elements. Jack also jokingly referred to Allie's pink and white polka dotted one-piece as her "Mother Teresa bathing suit."

Jack, with his curly dark brown hair, coffee-coloured skin, and mischievous brown eyes, looked like a young Lenny Kravitz. And his history as her brother's partner-in-crime made him seem like anything other than an appropriate authority figure. Allie profoundly resented the fact that she was going to have to spend the entire year feigning respect for Jack. Still, she was determined not to let either her mother's negativity or Jack's new coaching position dampen her excitement for the year ahead.

"What doesn't kill you makes you stronger. I am going to succeed no matter what," Allie told herself under her breath, praying her mother had not noticed that she was talking to herself once again.

When Allie arrived at the uniform shop, Lainey and Bailey were already there, being fitted for new blazers. As soon as they spotted Allie, the girls ran across the room and threw their arms around her. Sybilla said a polite hello to Bailey's mother and Lainey's father before bringing out her phone to check for work emails.

The three girls were ecstatic. They hadn't seen each other in weeks. Lainey had spent most of the summer with her mother's parents in Hong Kong, working on her Cantonese and Mandarin language skills. Meanwhile, Bailey traditionally spent most of the summer at her family's house in Hilton Head.

Once they stopped squealing joyously, the three young women began assessing each other for changes. Bailey was blonder. She claimed it was just from the sun *naturally* bleaching her hair, but Lainey and Allie knew better; they could tell when their friend had turned to a bottle for hair colour assistance. Of course, neither girl called Bailey on her bluff. They would never have embarrassed their friend like that.

Lainey looked much the same. She had a consistent look that involved tortoise-shell glasses and a shoulder-length black bob. Lainey had inherited her Chinese mother's hair and skin-tone, but she had her father's considerable height. Like her Swedish media mogul father, Hans Eriksson, Lainey was impressively tall. At five feet eight inches she towered over Allie, who was barely five-foot-two.

"Lainey, PLEASE stop growing," pleaded Allie. "You make me feel shorter and shorter every time I see you!"

"Oh come on, you know what you lack in height, you make up for in presence," replied Lainey. This was true. The girls had been debate partners since middle school, and while Lainey could force herself to stifle her nerves long enough to address an audience articulately, Allie could mesmerize a crowd with her passion. She could quote Eleanor Roosevelt or Sojourner Truth at the drop of a hat, and she seemed humanly incapable of ever admitting she was wrong. Of course, Allie *was* usually right.

"So, do you think Jack will let the two of you keep debating together?" asked Bailey as she walked over to a mirror to assess her appearance. She was pleased to note her blazer perfectly flattered her athletic frame. Bailey knew she was stirring up trouble with her question, but that was sort of the point. She honestly couldn't help herself. Bailey loved her friends, but she also enjoyed drama.

"I hope so. Do you think he might change things? Oh, why would he do that? We work so well together!" The very thought of losing Lainey as her debate partner made Allie panic. The two girls had won more tournaments together than any other ninth-grade team in Massachusetts' history. Allie and Lainey were a great pair. While Allie was a charismatic dynamo who saw "the big picture," Lainey's style was understated, but precise and incisive. Allie did not want to risk disaster by debating with someone else.

As Allie freaked out, speculating about whether Jack would let the girls stick with their partners from previous years, Lainey said nothing. She didn't want to admit it to her best friend, but she wasn't looking forward to debating again this year. Allie was simply too competitive for her, and it made Lainey anxious.

Just that spring, Lainey had vomited in the girls' washroom before a debate on affirmative action. She had been petrified of losing, of disappointing Allie, who was not just her teammate but her oldest and dearest friend. The stress was too much for the gentle Lainey to bear. Of course, she had yet to find the words to tell Allie that she really cared for her, and that she had enjoyed their time together on the debating team, but didn't want to continue their partnership for another school year. Lainey now feared she never would.

Eventually, once the debate talk was out of the way, the three girls fell into their usual rhythm of light hearted chatter about themselves and their classmates. They discussed who was dating whom, and Bailey triumphantly announced that she and her on-off boyfriend Austin had gotten back together the night before. Their gabbing lasted for approximately twenty minutes of uninterrupted speed talking. Their attention was only pulled away when the girls saw a mysterious twenty-something woman running across the courtyard from The Uniform Shop's big bay windows. She was a brunette of medium height and medium build. Though she had a cute face with beautifully full lips, it was difficult to focus on anything other than the fact that her navy blue J.Crew pencil skirt was on backwards.

"Who is that?" Lainey exclaimed in a judgmental tone. "What a total frump! She can't be one of the new teachers!"

"You can be a good teacher without dressing well," pointed out Lainey.

In a few moments, the harried woman had disappeared. They had no idea that just seven years before, that same woman stood where they were standing now, donning the same uniform. Her name was Anna Knole. She was the new guidance counsellor, and an ABC alumna. She was also running late for her very first meeting with Headmistress Carole.

3.

THIS ISN'T NEW YORK, THIS IS NEW ENGLAND

OCTAVIA FELT PRETTY SORRY for herself as she walked into the tenth grade locker room at Anne Bradstreet College. Even though she knew some girls found the first day of school absolutely thrilling, Octavia could muster no enthusiasm for it. She wanted to be at home, at a school where her boyfriend could pick her up each day. Unlike Octavia's father, Marcus did not have access to a G-6, so Boston was too far of a commute for him to make it by three-thirty, five days a week. Octavia had no idea how she was supposed to get through months on end without getting to kiss or cuddle with the boy she loved. It had been an absolute miracle that Marcus hadn't broken up with Octavia after the trouble her father had gotten Connor into for vandalizing the Robertsons' house.

Octavia remembered when Marcus called her for the first time after the debaucherous party that ruined her life. She was lying motionless on her bed in Montreal. Her parents were downstairs sitting across from each other at her mother's dining room table. They were discussing in very formal tones what they ought to "do" with their rebellious daughter. The words "boarding school" had been brought up more than once.

When Marcus's picture flashed up on her phone with his personalized ring tone, the opening bars of Lana Del Rey's "Young and Beautiful," Octavia's heart soared. Perhaps everything would be all right after all.

"Hey, babe," he drawled. "I know what happened with Connor and the police. I want you to know that I forgive you. Parents are tough." Marcus seemed to think he was being very chivalrous.

A small part of Octavia wondered why she needed to be forgiven. It was his friend who had vandalized a multi-million dollar summer home, not her. At the same time, she was relieved her boyfriend was not planning to hold a grudge. Besides, she needed his comfort too much to risk starting an argument.

"Where have you been, Marcus?" she croaked into her iPhone. "I needed you."

"I'm sorry, Babe. You know I really wanted to smoke some sheesha last night. You have that uptight rule about smoking in the house, so the guys and I had to leave. We hung out at Dave Holmes' cabin instead."

"Oh, cool." Octavia tried to sound like she wasn't pissed about having been abandoned for something so trivial. "Um, but why didn't you call or text?"

"My phone died and I didn't have my charger with me. I just got back to Montreal about a half hour ago."

"Yeah, okay…. But didn't any of the guys have a charger you could borrow? You all have the same phone, don't you?" Octavia asked quietly.

"All right, Sherlock, time to end this line of questioning. This is not like you. You're usually so chill." With that, Octavia decided not to push the issue further. She was relieved Marcus still wanted to be her boyfriend, and for now, it was enough to know she hadn't lost him. They made plans to sneak in some time together in a couple of days, when Sophie was at yoga. Little did Octavia know that, in approximately thirty-six hours, she'd be on a plane to Boston.

Not long after midnight, Octavia's parents roused their daughter to inform her she would spend the rest of the weekend packing. Mordecai had heard about Anne Bradstreet College from a work associate whose daughter had attended the school when she was a teen. All it took was one phone call, and Mordecai had finally found an answer to his daughter's teenage rebellion in the form of a Boston prep school. While primarily a day school, ABC had on-campus boarding facilities for the girls who came from out of town, and since Octavia knew no one who could be categorized as "a bad influence" in Boston, her parents decided it was the perfect solution. Of course, when she told Marcus, sobbing, he was less than thrilled. Marcus saw Octavia's departure as something of a betrayal. He didn't seem to understand that as a girl of fifteen, she had no choice.

Now, walking through the corridors of her new school, Octavia felt as if her situation were hopeless. She already knew she would never like ABC. She knew she would only ever resent it, and her parents, for separating her from the coolest guy she'd ever dated.

To make matters worse, Octavia usually started her day with a French Press coffee, but caffeine of all sorts was banned in the school's cafeteria. All there was to drink was water, fresh-squeezed orange juice, and a selection of herbal teas containing nettles and berries. The food was not much more exciting. Allie had a choice between quinoa pancakes and an egg-white omelette. She chose the omelette but every time it touched her lips, she wished it were a Montreal bagel with lox and cream cheese.

Octavia wondered, how was this sanitized place an American prep school? On television and in the movies, American prep schools were always just a front for kids who actually spent most of their time clubbing, having inappropriate sex with their teachers, and walking around in impractically high designer shoes. At ABC, there wasn't so much as a pair of Roger Vivier heels in sight!

The only girl at ABC Octavia had gotten to know so far was her roommate Su-Jin, a preppy girl from South Korea, who, when she wasn't playing squash, was permanently attached to her ear buds listening to Kendrick Lamar. Su-Jin didn't seem any more interested in making new friends than Octavia was. In light of this, the two girls rarely spoke to one another, though they had developed a silent respect for each other as fellow misanthropes.

As she searched for her locker on the morning of her first day of classes, Octavia cursed her terrible luck. She should have been in Montreal right now, living in her mom's ultra-modern house in The Plateau – the trendiest part of the city. And after school, she was supposed to be enjoying a cider in Mount Royal Park with Marcus. Octavia Irving was not meant to be living or going to school in a city famous for pilgrims!

As Octavia opened her locker and unpacked her school bags, she didn't even notice the three girls standing in a gaggle nearby, arguing over who they thought was the best character on *Girls*. As it happened, Lainey and Allie both favoured Shoshanna, because they found her combination of awkwardness and eccentricity to be relatable. Bailey, however, chose Marnie, primarily because she thought her to be the prettiest. They were about to start another debate over who they thought was the most interesting sister on *Downton Abbey*, when Allie suddenly noticed Octavia piling her books into an army green backpack with a pin on it that read, "ASK FIRST – SEX IS SUPPOSED TO BE FUN."

For her part, Allie Denning had never seen anyone like the person standing at the opposite end of the room. Octavia looked nothing like an ABC girl was meant to look. Her long dark hair was hanging along her face, dishevelled and loose. Allie doubted whether this new girl had so much as even run a brush through her tresses that morning. Allie also disapprovingly noted that Octavia was wearing a bright red American Apparel hoodie over her school blouse. A hoodie was certainly not part of the sanctioned uniform. Even worse, instead of wearing the regulation Mary Jane shoes, Octavia had on brown lace up Rag and Bone boots. Allie was dismayed to notice the contraband footwear wasn't even polished!

"Guys, look at that poor girl over there," Allie remarked to Lainey and Bailey. "She clearly just transferred here. I feel so bad. She has no idea how much trouble she is going to be in if she goes to class looking like some sort of ... hipster weirdo!" Horrified, Allie crossed the floor to say hello, and she hoped, to save this new girl from herself. Lainey and Bailey followed. Lainey because she was used to supporting her close friend of ten years in hair-brained schemes that often ended poorly, and Bailey because she could not bear to be left out of what she thought could be excellent gossip.

"Excuse me, I do not think we have met. You must be new to ABC. I'm Alexandra Denning. Most people call me Allie though. What's your name?" Allie extended her hand to shake the new girl's.

Octavia looked sceptically over at Allie and her friends, who were a vision of the perfect ABC uniform. Their navy blue blazers were neatly starched, their skirts were exactly regulation length, and their patent leather Mary Jane shoes were freshly polished to the point of gleaming. Octavia accepted Allie's extended hand but shook it half-heartedly. What kind of a fifteen-year-old girl SHAKES HANDS? Octavia wondered. She was clearly in the presence of the class goody-goody, who, by the looks of it, presided over a friendship circle of narcs. Octavia made a mental note never to ask Allie or her friends which bars in Boston accepted fake IDs.

"I'm Octavia," she replied, before turning her attention once more to unpacking her backpack.

Allie was not discouraged by the new girl's chilly demeanour. "And where are you from?" she asked, using the formal tone she usually reserved for dealing with teachers and Kennedys.

"I moved here from Quebec a couple of days ago. I just transferred from Miss Edmonds' and Miss Collins' School in Montreal."

Lainey, who had always been shy around new people, was standing silently with her hands by her sides. She wished Allie were not so committed to welcoming strangers.

Bailey, however, decided to enter the conversation with full force. "So Octavia, interesting name," Bailey said in a tone Octavia thought was somewhat patronizing. "What brings you to ABC? Did you decide to transfer because of our excellent reputation with the Ivies? ABC is one of Harvard's favoured prep schools..."

"No," responded Octavia firmly. "I didn't want to transfer, and I plan on going to McGill, 'The Harvard of the North,' like my boyfriend."

"That's funny, considering *Harvard* is the *Harvard of the North*," shot back Bailey while flashing what Octavia was pretty sure was an insincere smile.

Allie could see the hostility brewing in Octavia's eyes. It was clear she was not amused by Bailey's comments, and even Allie, who considered Dartmouth to be a safety school, had to admit they were pretty condescending. "I'm sure McGill is a very good college, Bailey," commented Allie in an attempt to defuse the awkwardness. "And Octavia, you'll really get to like ABC," she added for good measure. "It's a very close-knit community and the teachers are great. You'll fit right in."

Octavia nodded. She was starting to warm up to Allie. Then Allie ruined their connection by issuing the following admonishment: "I must say, however, that you should really be wearing the proper uniform to make a good impression."

"Um, what do you mean 'make a good impression?'" asked Octavia, rolling her eyes. "Who am I trying to impress?"

"Well, it's your first day. Don't you want your teachers to think you're a good student?" Allie seemed to think her logic was obvious.

"What does my uniform have to do with my intellect?" asked a puzzled Octavia.

Allie was taken aback by the question but decided to push on with her line of argumentation. "Well, it doesn't have anything to do with your academic abilities per se. But you want to show ABC teachers and administrators you take school seriously. Wearing the proper uniform is symbolic of that."

"Look, do you think they'll give me lower marks on my finals because I'm not wearing the correct shoes?"

"No! ABC teachers would never tamper with a student's test results for any reason. Marks are sacred!" Allie could not believe anyone would dare ask such a question.

"Well then, I might as well wear what I like. What are they going to do, give me a detention? I already live at the school anyway." Octavia reached down and swung her backpack onto her shoulder, ready to be on her way

"Look," interjected Bailey in an authoritative tone before Octavia could leave. "That kind of ... ensemble might be accepted elsewhere, but we're very strict about the uniform here. We don't wear Christmas sweaters in September, and boots like that are best left to the dirty hipsters of Bushwick. This isn't New York, this is New England."

Octavia said nothing. She gave the three young women her signature withering stare, then turned on her Rag & Bone boots, and walked away.

Octavia was sitting in an office that did not look fully set up. There were boxes scattered across the floor, and degrees from Yale and Harvard, displayed in imposing gilded frames, lay un-hung on the desk. There was a stapler on the sofa, and an open, half-eaten package of M&Ms on an end table near the door. Octavia thought the space resembled her bedroom back in Montreal. The weird part was this office belonged to Anna Knole, ABC's new guidance counsellor. Octavia wondered what kind of wisdom this woman could offer if her office was as messy as the average sixteen-year-old's bedroom.

Anna was seated awkwardly behind her disorganized desk. She seemed self-conscious, as though she knew her office looked as if it had just been the target of a drone strike. Maybe she's planning on cleaning up later, thought Octavia.

"Sorry. I promise my office won't usually look like this. I was a last-minute hire and I'm still putting things away," Anna said, blushing. This was partially true. The previous guidance counsellor had quit eighteen days before the school year to run off with one of her students' fathers, whom she'd met at a parent/teacher conference. They were now sunning themselves on a beach in Bermuda. Even if this emergency situation had not transpired, however, it was still unlikely Anna's office would have been any neater. Though brilliantly educated and hardworking, Anna had never mastered the art of organizing her files or hiding her candy in drawers.

"Anyway, Octavia, I see the marks from your old school in Montreal are somewhat … inconsistent." Anna was outwardly diplomatic, while secretly thinking to herself that this girl's family must have given ABC a very sizeable donation to secure her admission.

"Oh yeah," agreed Octavia nonchalantly. "A lot of the stuff they teach you at school just isn't for me." Octavia was calm and casual. She was not at all self-conscious about her diverse academic record. "I mean, when am I going to need something like chemistry in real life?"

"Well, I suppose if you do not want to be an engineer, a pharmacist, a doctor or a chemist, you are probably fine on that one." Anna punctuated her statement with a raised eyebrow. "However, you're probably going to need English. I know that because we are speaking the language right now."

Octavia immediately became defensive. "It's not my fault I didn't do well in English last year. My teacher was really stuffy and super boring. I love to read, but she was so conservative. She never let us study any women authors, which is ridiculous because Charlotte Brontë is every bit as talented as Charles Dickens." Octavia now spoke with a level of conviction Anna couldn't help but respect.

"Octavia, I am going to level with you. Your file says you want to go to McGill in Montreal." Octavia nodded in agreement. "Well, you are going to need a much higher GPA to get in there. The only subjects you had As in last year are French, music and Latin. You have Bs and Cs in everything else except for gym, where you have a D!"

"The D in gym was not my fault." Octavia once again became defensive. "I skipped the class most days in protest. They tried to force us to wear these completely unflattering polyester shorts."

Anna was about to respond to her student's sartorial gripes when there came a knock at the door. It was a jaunty knock. The sort of knock made by a person who is awfully excited to see someone.

"Hello?" Anna called out tentatively. She really hoped it was not Headmistress Carole checking up on her.

"It's Rajeev Lahiri," responded a deep and sexy voice. The door opened to reveal an exceedingly attractive man in his early thirties. He was wearing grey cords, a white polo shirt, and a navy blue blazer. His smile was wide, his teeth impossibly white

"Oh, hello," said Anna. Octavia noticed her guidance counsellor was blushing again. "Is there something I can help you with?"

"No, I just came to say hi. I heard a rumour you were working here now but I needed to see it for myself." His gaze was so focused on Anna that Octavia was pretty sure this Rajeev Lahiri person hadn't even noticed she was in the room.

"Well, it's really me. In the flesh ... er, I mean, in person. You know what I mean." What the hell was going on here? Octavia wanted to *know*.

After an awkward thirty seconds that seemed like an eternity, Anna and Rajeev stopped staring at each other and came back down to earth. "Actually, I'm just with a student now." Anna gestured over to Octavia's seat. "Why don't we catch up at lunch?"

"I look forward to it." Rajeev paused for a few moments before finally turning away, as if he could not bear to let Anna out of his sight. After Rajeev left, Anna remarked, "That's Mr. Lahiri. He's actually going to be your history teacher. I know him because he used to be a student teacher way back when I was in twelfth grade right here at ABC." Her tone was excessively cheery and bright, as if to distract from the awkwardly intimate moment that had just transpired in front of a new student.

"Oh. He must have been your favourite student teacher," said Octavia dryly.

Octavia was still confused about what had unfolded between her guidance counsellor and her new American history teacher. If Anna had not seemed so awkward and inept, she would have accused her of flirting! The idea of two teachers chatting each other up shook Octavia to her very core, as she had always considered her educators to be emotionless drones who probably slept at the desks in their classrooms. Still, even she had to admit Anna and Rajeev would make something of an adorable couple.

Of course, there was also the unusual fact that Mr. Lahiri had been Ms. Knole's teacher seven years before. This did not strike Octavia as so bizarre. She prided herself on being very European in her outlook on romance. She was fond of declaring dramatically, "You cannot control who you fall in love with!" She was definitely on team Angie and Brad. At the same time, Octavia was certain that most of the Bostonites she'd just met would disapprove of affairs between students and teachers. Had Octavia completely imagined the chemistry between the two adults in that office? Or did these people share a history that was somewhat less wholesome than learning about The Boston Tea Party?

Octavia's reverie was interrupted when Anna finally regained her focus once and for all. Returning to guidance counsellor mode, Anna put on a serious expression. "So, Octavia, you'll need to try harder academically if you want to get into the school of your choice, but another thing you'll need to do is get involved in extra-curriculars."

Octavia snorted with undisguised disgust, but Anna continued. "So, do you like any sports?"

"I play tennis sometimes, but not seriously. I mostly like it for the outfits. I don't *do* sweat."

"Okay, how about the Textile Arts Club?" Anna ventured.

"I like crafts but I'm not crafty. I have a credit card. I can buy stuff on Etsy instead."

"Drama Club?"

"I don't want to have to wear a wig," shot back Octavia snappily.

"Well, you do seem good at refuting all of my suggestions. How about something where we can harness that argumentative spirit, like the debate team?" Anna knew this last suggestion was her 'Hail Mary' pass.

"Are you kidding? Stuff like that is for nerds who care about things like who the Prime Minister of Belgium is!"

Anna paused, looking Octavia straight in the eye before saying, "Octavia, I think you actually *do* care about who the Prime Minister of Belgium is. I think you care about a lot more than you realize, and you should definitely sign up for Debate Team tryouts. I want you to go, and I want you to put in some effort. If you don't make it on, I promise I won't bother you about extra-curriculars for the rest of term. Deal?"

Octavia was irritated at being railroaded like this. No one had ever tried to make her get seriously involved in an activity before. Her parents didn't seem to care what she did, with the exception of when she threw alcohol-fuelled benders at the country house.

Sophie and Morty had never spent much time moulding their daughter into an accomplished young woman. They had, overall, been easy on Octavia, keeping their expectations low, barely batting an eye when she brought home mediocre report cards. Now, in Anna's office, for the first time in fifteen years, someone was asking her to *really* apply herself. It felt inconvenient, but, at the same time, a little part of Octavia liked the idea of an adult believing she was capable of more than putting together trendy outfits.

At lunch, Octavia waited until she thought no one was looking. Once she believed the coast was clear, she approached the bulletin board outside the school's central office where the signup sheet for debate team tryouts was posted. Just as Octavia had finished printing her name, however, a tall blonde girl approached with a quizzical look on her face.

"*You're* signing up for debate tryouts?" spat the attractive young woman, curling one of her luscious locks around her pointer finger.

Octavia was equal parts defensive and embarrassed. "What do you care?"

"Oh, I can recognize a kindred spirit when I see one," she replied, gesturing to Octavia's feet. "No one with that kind of footwear wants to hang out with a bunch of prissy teachers' pets who get excited at debating electoral college reform." She paused to give a mean-spirited smirk. "You know, it's not too late to cross your name of the list."

Octavia said nothing. She didn't want to be considered a nerd on the first day at her new school, but she was surprised to find a small part of her really didn't want to disappoint Miss Knole.

"Oh, I'm just going to get my guidance counsellor off my back. She wants me to 'get involved,' whatever that means. I don't actually intend to TRY!" Octavia affected a nonchalant tone. With a toss of her glossy dark tendrils, she added, "I'm Octavia, by the way. I just got shipped here from Montreal by my killjoy parents."

The pretty blonde girl grinned mischievously. "I'm Imogene Butler-Thompson. And I know ALL ABOUT outsmarting killjoy parents. I think you and I are going to be good friends. Why don't we go to Starbucks and get to know each other better over lattes after school?"

Octavia readily agreed. She was delighted by the prospect of making a friend with common interests, even if those were only talking smack about good girls and consuming caffeinated beverages. Octavia was worried, however, that their friendship might deteriorate if she actually made the debate team. What would happen if she suddenly got involved and became one of those girls her prospective friend liked to mock? She didn't want that to happen, but, at the same time, something inside Octavia worried that, when the time came for the tryout, she wouldn't be able to stop herself from doing the best she could.

4.

TEACHERS CAN HAVE CRUSHES TOO

ANNA SPEED-WALKED all the way to the staff lounge. It was a sunny room full of antique wood furniture and oil paintings depicting significant events in Boston's history. The lounge was where teachers typically ate their lunches, safely out of students' reach.

This lunch hour, Anna was not particularly hungry. She had just finished a package of M&Ms back in her office. However, she figured she could force herself to eat a salad for appearances' sake. After all, it would look strange to sit in the lunchroom at lunchtime without any food. It would be a little too obvious she had ulterior motives.

Against her better judgment, Anna was unabashedly excited to reconnect with Rajeev. She vividly remembered the first time she met the man she referred to then as Mr. Lahiri. She was in twelfth grade and Rajeev was completing his student teacher training at ABC.

Instead of exuding nerves as most student teachers do, Rajeev possessed a magnetic persona that made students respect him immediately. Then, when Mr. Lahiri informed the class his undergraduate thesis at Amherst had been written on the history of Boston speakeasies during prohibition, his coolness cred went off the charts. He also had tickets to an upcoming Killers concert, which made the seventeen-year-old Anna swoon on the inside.

Rajeev was the best teacher Anna had ever had, despite the

fact that he was technically still learning himself. He emboldened her to write essays on controversial topics that interested her, such as Margaret Sanger's quest for safe and legal birth control. Anna learned that while Sanger was a proponent of women's reproductive rights, she also believed in using birth control for the purposes of eugenics, thus problematizing her legacy considerably. It was assignments like this, which, under Rajeev's tutelage, taught Anna the world was not a simple place.

It had now been years since Rajeev and Anna last spoke. So much had changed. Anna had an undergraduate degree from Yale and a Master's degree from Harvard. In addition, she was also a newly minted dropout of MIT's PhD program in psychology.

When Anna dropped out, she told all of her friends and family she had merely taken a year off from academia, but in reality, she knew she could never face returning. Something happened at MIT that Anna could never erase. It was something she deeply regretted, even though, in rare moments of clarity, she was fairly certain it was not her fault.

When Anna arrived in the staff room, Rajeev was seated alone at one of the round oak dining tables. He was deep in thought, reading a copy of that morning's *The New York Times*. Anna almost felt guilty interrupting. She loved the furrow in Rajeev's brow as he concentrated, but she loved the sound of Rajeev's deep, silky voice even more.

"Hi!" Anna said brightly.

"Hello," replied Rajeev, putting down the paper. "How is the first morning of school treating you?"

"Well, *school* is easy; I'm starting to realize it's the students who make it so hard," she quipped.

"Yep, they will break your heart. Today, a girl in my ninth grade history class asked me if Jonathon Swift was famous for being related to Taylor Swift."

"Oh, Good Lord! How did you keep yourself from laughing?" Anna giggled.

"It was very hard to keep a straight face. But I keep reminding myself that they're young. They're just learning. It's not their fault they don't know all the answers yet. It's my job to teach them, so that when they grow up, they know better," Rajeev replied, making Anna's heart soar in what she knew was an unprofessional manner.

"So, Anna, have you decided which extra-curricular you plan on supervising yet?"

"Oh God, I totally forgot that all ABC faculty are required to supervise at least one extra-curricular." Anna began to panic. She could not believe she had completely neglected such an important aspect of her job description.

"Well, if you aren't committed to anything yet, I could really use some help supervising the debate team. Your predecessor used to do that, but then she ran off with one of Mitt Romney's cousins and left me in the lurch," explained Rajeev.

"What would this job entail?" asked Anna, eyes sparkling. She was trying to suppress her excitement at the thought of working closely with Rajeev. It would be a challenge.

"Well, we have this kid from Harvard who'll do most of the coaching. He won the high school debate nationals last year. His name's Jack Mansbridge. His father is Headmaster at Hillsview."

"Okay, so then what would *we* do?" enquired Anna, trying to keep the suggestiveness out of her voice.

"Well, we would sit in the back of the classroom bantering to one another while Jack leads training sessions." Rajeev was now sporting what some might call a saucy grin. "Oh, and we get to chaperone them when they go to tournaments," he added. "Sometimes that's only as exotic as a trip to Roxbury Latin School, but once I got to attend a public speaking tournament in Prague, which was awesome."

"Okay, I'd love to!" exclaimed Anna. "I was more of a school play-slash-year book girl when I was at ABC, but if debate has an opening, I'd be happy to help out."

"Perfect," declared Rajeev enthusiastically.

Just then, as if on cue, a slender woman in her late twenties approached Rajeev from behind and placed her hands on his shoulders. "Hello, my dear," said the interloper in a Parisian accent. Anna couldn't help but notice this woman was the epitome of French elegance. She wore an understated light pink smock dress with a yellow and white silk scarf tied neatly around her neck. Her red hair shone in the light streaming through the nearby bay windows.

In a matter of seconds, the pretty French woman had taken up residence in a chair on Rajeev's left hand side. He was now sandwiched between her and Anna.

For a few awkward moments, Rajeev said nothing, but then the beautiful French woman prompted him to speak by way of elbowing him in the stomach. "Aren't you going to introduce us?"

"Oh, of course," responded a startled Rajeev. "Anna, this is Melissa Marcel. She's one of our best French teachers," Rajeev punctuated his introduction by motioning to the comely young woman.

"I may be only *one* of the best French teachers at ABC, Rajeev, that is true, but I am definitely the best girlfriend you have ever had!" Melissa emphasized her decree by grabbing Rajeev's hand in a display of ownership. Anna was pretty sure Melissa was issuing a warning sign to stay away from her man.

Anna tried to hide her surprise. "Oh, how nice to meet you, Melissa! I've heard so much about you from the girls already," she lied. Anna was not sure why she felt the need to be dishonest about this. Up until now, she had not even known this glamourous French uber-babe existed, but Anna needed something coherent to say to prove she was not taken aback. This particular falsehood was the first thought that sprang to mind.

Not knowing what else to say, Anna began to turn red. Every inch of her screamed to flee. She wanted to escape the judgmental gaze of the world's best-looking French teacher, a woman who just happened to be running her enchanting green eyes critically over Anna's fairly ordinary face.

Anna was cute. She knew she was cute and usually wasn't particularly self-conscious about her appearance.

Now everyone knows that being cute has its benefits. A cute girl is rarely so intimidating that a potential love interest feels too frightened to approach. Cute is welcoming and sweet. People are not typically jealous of the cute girl. She flies under the radar with her propensity to trip a little bit more often than an elegant woman would, and the fact her hair is never completely in place. Anna knew all this and usually felt happy to be a moderately attractive, normal-looking woman. Looks had never been her priority in the past.

By contrast to Anna's serviceably pleasant features, however, Melissa had a beauty so polished Anna was pretty sure she could see her reflection in the woman's alabaster skin. And the reflection Anna saw made her believe she was not the type of girl who could ever compete with Melissa. Anna spent the rest of lunch hour in a haze of her own insecurity as she lamented how much better everything sounded when you had the same accent as Marion Cotillard.

Allie and Jack were in the process of getting everything prepared for the Debate Team tryouts the next day, but as ever, they were butting heads. It was three-forty-five p.m. Because of a staff meeting that afternoon, the faculty supervisors could not attend, leaving Allie and Jack to argue in peace in the privacy of ABC's Debates Room.

The Debates Room was a great hall that had been constructed over a century and a half ago with a helpful donation from Henry Joseph Gardner. Gardner was a former governor of Massachusetts whose daughters and granddaughters all attended ABC. The room was initially intended to house giant quilting bees, but in response to the women's liberation movement of the 1960s, what had previously been known as the "Handi-craft Hall" became known as the "Anne Bradstreet College Debates Room."

The large, oak-panelled room had a vaulted ceiling with phenomenal acoustics. Photographs of famous individuals who had spoken at ABC adorned its walls. It was an impressive collection, boasting such illustrious personages as Jackie Kennedy Onassis, Queen Noor, Elizabeth Bishop, Jane Goodall, Nancy Pelosi, Hillary Clinton, Anita Hill, Wendy Wasserstein, Ruth Bader Ginsburg, and Sonia Sotomayor.

The Debates Room was without doubt Allie's favourite place at ABC, and perhaps in the whole world. Standing there, a place where so many strong and capable women had spoken before her, Allie felt as if anything were possible if she only worked hard enough. In this space, Allie believed all of her dreams were within reach.

Feeling emboldened by being in her element, Allie was even more assertive than usual with Jack. "I don't like the speech topics you've prepared. They aren't serious enough for something as important as debate tryouts," declared Allie confidently.

"Define serious." Jack never missed a chance to challenge her.

"You know what I mean. I want topics that force people to prove they know things about the world. A sound knowledge of current events is essential for debating," Allie said forcefully.

"Look, Al, I know what I'm doing. I am a former High School National Debating Champion." Jack pulled rank. As accomplished as she was, Allie had not yet reached the lofty heights Jack achieved in his senior year.

Of course, Jack also knew Allie would one day become a far better debater than he was, but for the time being, it was convenient to lord his success over her when he wanted Allie to listen. It was the most effective teaching tactic available to him.

"Allie," said Jack plaintively. "You know as well as I do that people can learn more about current events if we teach them; however, it is much harder to teach someone charisma and presence."

Allie nodded slightly in response. She knew Jack was right but she was not crazy about the idea of admitting it. He continued his lecture: "If we keep the topics accessible, it will be easier to identify talent. I don't want to end up with a bunch of new recruits who can point out the capitol of Yemen on a map but are incapable of modulating their voices."

"You mean Sana'a?" she teased.

Jack responded with a confused stare.

"Sana'a is the capitol of Yemen," Allie declared triumphantly.

"All right, you know what we do with smart-aleck Allies." Jack had a mischievous glint in his eyes. Ever since Allie was little, whenever she obnoxiously corrected someone about anything (and she corrected people a lot), Jack and Aram would grab her and tickle her until she begged for mercy.

Allie raised an eyebrow. "You wouldn't dare defile a room that has hosted Hillary Rodham Clinton herself by starting a tickle fight." Allie stood her ground across from Jack, refusing to move one muscle. She displayed no fear whatsoever as Jack inched closer to where she stood, his deep brown eyes fixed on her hazel gaze.

Jack raised his pointer finger and pressed it gently against Allie's mouth as if to say, "Shhh." Then he used one arm to grab Allie by the shoulders while he tickled her enthusiastically with his free hand.

Allie had been tickled by Jack hundreds of times before, but never without Aram there. Previously, she had found these tickle attacks completely annoying. Today, however, she did not feel desperate for it to stop.

Jack was holding Allie by the shoulder with his left hand while tickling her all over her torso with the other. His mouth was so close that Allie could feel his warm breath on her face. Jack smelled clean and fresh, like Ivory soap. Allie felt a rush of warmth fill her whole body, like she'd just come back from a long run in the noonday sun. What was this feeling? she wondered. Her heartbeat quickened and her skin tingled. Allie had never felt so aware of her body before.

Jack continued to tickle Allie vigorously until they were interrupted by the sound of Allie's iPhone ringing. When he heard her vintage telephone ringtone, Jack immediately released Allie from his grip. It was as though a spell had been broken. Sybilla was on the other end of the line.

"Allie!" cried Sybilla into her mouthpiece. "I have been sitting in the ABC parking lot waiting for you for ten whole minutes. Come out immediately! Contrary to what you may think, I have better things to do than chauffeur my fifteen-year-old daughter around at her convenience."

"Sorry, Mom. I lost track of time. I'll be right there," stammered Allie. She ended the conversation with her mother and began frantically gathering her things.

"I have to go," Allie told Jack without looking at him. "I'm late. My mom is waiting for me and you know how she hates waiting."

"Tell Sybilla it was my fault. Tell her I said you couldn't leave until everything was done," Jack offered. He knew what Allie's mother was like when she felt her time was being wasted.

"Thank you, but I can handle this situation myself." Before he knew it, Allie had rushed out the door.

5.
MIC DROP AT DEBATE TRYOUTS

IT WAS THE AFTERNOON of the debate team tryouts. A total of thirty-three young women were trying out for ten spots. It was going to be a competitive and stressful day full of complicated decisions, but Allie Denning did not mind that at all.

Allie knew being captain of the ABC Debate Team was a huge responsibility, but she savoured that feeling. Being in charge and doing things right was an area in which she excelled. She was the kind of girl who even remembered to floss between meals, so Allie was fairly certain she could handle anything.

There was, however, something that seemed odd to Allie about the list of girls vying for a coveted spot on the ABC Debate Team: Octavia Irving was one of them. Now, Allie had nothing in particular against Octavia. If a girl chose to violate rules regarding the uniform and did not seem to pay much attention in math class that was her prerogative. Of course, such choices were not very becoming of a young woman at a school as prestigious as ABC, but Allie grudgingly admitted it was none of her business to care about that. Allie had offered her friendly advice to Octavia the day they first met, but Octavia had rebuffed her. Allie was not one to chase down the friendship of young women who rejected her overtures.

Still, Allie felt it had to be said that a girl like Octavia just would not fit in on the ABC Debate Team. Allie had always thought of debating as an extra curricular for *good girls* like her, the kind of girls who did their homework diligently and only had time to watch television on the weekends. By contrast, Allie suspected Octavia was the type of girl who never did homework and spent her weekends attempting to sneak into the kinds of bars at which indie rock bands perform.

Allie knew she should try to resist feelings of prejudice, but she was confident she already knew enough about Octavia Irving to pass judgment. Her judgment was that Octavia was the kind of girl who did not seem to care about anything important, least of all her future.

As the girls flooded the ABC Debates Room to commence tryouts, Jack informed them of the rules. "All right, so right now we are just testing you on speaking and thinking ability. We will not be doing formal debates today. It is our philosophy that the mechanics of debating can be taught, but raw talent cannot be," said Jack in his grownup voice.

He sounded so serious, thought Allie. You would never guess this was the same guy who'd tickled her for several minutes the day before.

Allie and Jack sat at the front of the room behind an imposing oak desk, their iPads in hand to take notes on each girl's performance. Anna and Rajeev stood off to the side. They were there primarily to supervise and make sure no one lit anything on fire. They deferred to Jack and Allie to make all the difficult decisions.

Allie hated to admit it, as she wanted the ABC Debate Team to be as strong as possible, but most of the speeches she heard were lackluster at best.

First, there was the girl who droned on and on about how hard it is to look after her pony, Marigold. Next came the boarding student from Frankfurt who proclaimed, "I hate knitting. Why do it when you can just buy a sweater at the store? Knitting is inefficient, like Poland!" Jack and Allie were concerned about the xenophobic nature of her argumentation.

Later came a ninth-grader who never uttered a word. She simply burst into tears as soon as she reached the podium, standing there weeping awkwardly for about thirty seconds. Miss Knole had to escort her out of the room to recover from the traumatic experience.

Octavia was one of the last speakers of the day. When her turn came, she approached confidently to retrieve a topic from Jack's Red Sox cap. He playfully referred to the cap as his "debating sorting cup." The subject on the piece of paper Octavia fished out was "All the World's A Stage." Octavia was meant to deliver a five-minute speech based on those words, explaining what they meant to her. Octavia felt nervous as she scanned the room, her reality suddenly dawning on her. She examined the girls of ABC, their shiny black patent shoes and skirts that reached the tips of their fingers within a millimetre. She felt their eyes on her, too. She caught Allie's glance, as Allie stood at the ready, iPad in hand, wearing a neutral expression on her face.

Allie was fairly certain that Octavia had decided to tryout in order to make a mockery of the whole process. Allie half expected her to moon everyone part way through her speech. This was one girl who simply was not up to the task. Or so Allie thought.

Octavia shook off their stares. When her two minutes of preparation time were over, Octavia strode gracefully to the podium. Her posture was erect, and she wore an uncharacteristically serious expression. Allie was a little bit freaked out by the sudden change in Octavia's posture and steely, focused gaze. It almost seemed as if Octavia were *trying*.

"All the world's a stage ... and all the men and women merely players!" declared Octavia as she threw her arms up in the air dramatically. "This is a quotation by William Shakespeare, one of the most important writers in the history of the English language."

Allie was surprised Octavia recognized the quotation was by

Shakespeare. Of course, he was one of Allie's favourite authors, but it had never occurred to her that a girl who couldn't be bothered to brush her hair in the morning would invest hours of her life into reading *Hamlet*. She had not taken Octavia for the kind of person who familiarized herself with classic literature.

"Shakespeare may have written these words centuries ago, but the sentiment remains true today. We are all of us just actors, playing a part. Everyone from Barack Obama to the Kardashians pretends to be someone they are not. Everyone has an image, the way they want to be seen, or the way they think they ought to behave."

The room was so silent Allie really did think she may have heard a pin – probably a bobby pin from another student's hair – drop. Octavia was managing to hold everyone's attention with aplomb.

"What would happen if we were truly free to be ourselves? If we were free to act as we wished to, not as we thought we had to? In high school more so than maybe anywhere else, we are beholden to the stereotypes we're expected to perform." Here, Octavia paused and gave a meaningful look at Allie, who refused to meet her gaze.

"Some of us are the jocks, while others are the hipster kids who love Arcade Fire but can't admit they listen to Taylor Swift in secret shame. There are the popular kids who worry if they miss one party they'll be considered nerds, and there are the nerds who worry if they go to a party, people won't take them seriously anymore." Allie bristled. How *dare* she claim to understand nerds? Octavia, however, was not done yet.

"What would happen, however, if we all stopped behaving as expected for one day? If we all stopped being who we thought the script of life expected us to be?" There was a thoughtful look in Octavia's eyes. "I don't know what would happen if we all decided to be who we really want to be, but I know it would be interesting. Thank you."

As she finished her speech, Octavia gave a triumphant smile.

In a dramatic flourish, she even dropped the mic as she left the stage.

Allie was flabbergasted.

"Well, obviously Octavia made the team," said Jack matter-of-factly. He and Allie were seated at a nearby Legal Seafood location eating crab cakes. Allie had wanted to finish the decision-making process at school, but Jack insisted he was too hungry to concentrate. He was also decidedly sick of Harvard cafeteria dinners.

"Yes, I suppose we have to," conceded Allie, dipping her crab cake into the extra remoulade sauce she had ordered on the side. "Her speech was good."

"Good? That's a bit of an understatement. Octavia was by far the best person we saw. Hell, after you, she may even be the best person we have on the team."

"Excuse me, but I believe that's going a bit far, Jack."

"I don't think it is. A lot of the school's best speakers graduated last year. Look, I know you are beyond brilliant, but we need to get you a standout partner. If we don't, all of your talent is going to be wasted," said Jack, reaching across the table to give Allie a comforting pat on the shoulder. Was he patronizing her? Allie was incensed.

"I have a 'standout' partner, remember? I have always debated with Lainey," said Allie, trying to choke back a possible onset of tears.

"I know. You guys did well in junior debating, but the senior level is more competitive. Lainey is a genius, but I think you know her heart isn't into it like yours is. Do you think she really wants to devote the time it would take to becoming the best team in America?

Allie said nothing. She just glared at jack.

"Allie, you can give me the silent treatment, but there is no point remaining in denial on this one. We've both known Lainey for years. You know her real dream is to become editor of

The ABC Newspaper. I can't force someone to be as passionate about debate as you are."

"And you think Octavia Irving is passionate about it?" spat an infuriated Allie. She wasn't sure if she was angry because she knew Jack was wrong, or because he could just be right.

"Yes, I do. I think she loves speaking in front of a crowd."

"Lainey is hardworking. She knows about current events. Octavia can't even get it together to put her uniform on properly! She is not going to take debating seriously, Jack. Plus, she has no experience whatsoever." Allie was on the verge of sobbing, and feared that she was beginning to sound whiney. There were tears in her eyes she was desperately trying to blink back. How could Jack even contemplate pairing her with the troublemaking likes of Octavia Irving?

"You're right, Octavia doesn't have experience, but you do. You can help her. It will be worth it, Allie, I promise."

"How do you know that, Jack?"

"Because she has something that I can't teach," he replied.

"And what is that?"

"Octavia has presence."

"And don't I?" Allie felt hurt. She was certain Jack was comparing her to Octavia in his head, finding Octavia's contraband lipstick and wild curls preferable to her carefully calculated preppiness.

"Of course you have presence, Allie. You are one of the most eloquent and compelling speakers I have ever met in my life." Jack had no idea why Allie Denning, who was such a dynamo, would doubt her considerable talent. He didn't see Octavia as a threat to Allie at all. He saw her as an asset.

"If I have so much presence, why can't I debate with Lainey anymore? Maybe she seems a little unenthusiastic sometimes. Still, if I'm really that good, surely my speaking ability will make up for her occasional lack of passion." Allie was pleading. She was embarrassed to be grovelling in front of Jack Mansbridge, but she had exhausted every other option.

Jack surveyed Allie's face. Her cheeks were red with emotion. He felt a pang in his stomach. He hadn't meant to hurt Allie, but he was more experienced. He knew he was doing the right thing.

Jack took a deep breath. "I'm sorry, I have to pull rank. Lainey and Bailey are less interested in this activity and should therefore be each other's debate partners this year. I'm in charge. This is ultimately my decision. ABC is paying me to put together the best possible pairings, and I know that you and Octavia belong together." Jack felt a twinge of guilt as he looked into Allie's eyes. They were glistening with tears on the verge of spilling. He hated the thought of making her weep, and yet, he knew he was doing the right thing for her. Jack had Allie's best interests at heart. If he hadn't, he would not have bothered fighting her on the issue at all.

"Excuse me," said Allie abruptly. She got up from the table and ran to the ladies' room. There was no way Jack Mansbridge was going to see her cry into her crab cakes.

6.

FRENCH TEACHERS CAN BE MEAN GIRLS TOO

A FTER SHE WAS FINISHED supervising the debate try-outs, Anna Knole quickly jumped into the Prius her parents gave her as a gift for completing her Master's degree. She was racing home to change before an evening out. She could not wait to exchange her appropriate navy blue J.Crew pencil skirt and heels for some jeans, a T-shirt, and her favourite pair of Tom's shoes. Unfortunately, Anna did not have time to reapply her makeup. She knew her mascara was a little smudged, but she was already running late to meet her best friend Carlos. For Anna, beauty was far less important than punctuality.

Anna and Carlos met when they were both in their first year at Yale. They sat beside each other in Introduction to Sociology. Carlos' father was a former vice-president of Mexico, and one of the country's wealthiest citizens. His family probably had more money than God, but despite this, Carlos was fairly down-to-earth. He made a point of bragging about how unlike his cousins he was. While they all had chauffeured Bentleys, he drove a comparatively modest Mercedes S-Class. Carlos even had an actual job working as an architect for a high-end property developer in Boston.

Unspeakably hip, Carlos and his DJ boyfriend Anton lived in a gorgeous converted warehouse. The building was so cool Anna did not even feel trendy enough to enter it unless she was wearing something recently purchased from an independent fashion designer name Gillian, pronounced with a hard "G," off Etsy.

"You're late," said Carlos as Anna approached the entrance to the Westland Ave. Whole Foods where they had agreed to meet. Carlos had been waiting for fifteen minutes.

"I know, I'm sorry. I would have texted, but I take that law about texting and driving very seriously. These debate tryouts at school ended late, and then I had to rush home to change. So of course traffic just had to be a nightmare too!" Anna was self-conscious. She hated being late, yet sometimes her life was so scattered and disorganized it happened anyway.

"Okay, don't worry about it. I forgive you, my Anna Banana. Let's go shopping for some organic dips."

A few minutes later, Anna and Carlos were deciding which brand of hummus to bring to their feminist book club meeting. It was at this precise moment when Melissa Marcel suddenly appeared from behind a large display of gourmet cheeses.

"Hello, Anna!" said Melissa in a tone a little too enthusiastic to be genuine.

"Hi, Melissa," Anna replied in what she hoped was a calm and collected voice. Despite her best efforts, Anna still felt awkward when confronted with the woman Rajeev was dating.

"So, is this your boyfriend?" asked Melissa, gesturing toward Carlos.

"Ha! No, I have never dated anyone with breasts," said Carlos archly. "I must say, I love everything you're wearing. That is such an elegant trench coat. Is it Burberry?" asked Carlos, thumbing the checkered upturned collar of her coat with an appreciative nod. High fashion was one of his hobbies. He was a regular at Paris Fashion Week. When you had the kind of money he did, Tom Ford suits seemed like a good deal.

"Why yes, it is vintage Burberry. Your friend has a very good eye, Anna." Melissa punctuated her statement with a wide smile that revealed perfectly even, perfectly white teeth. "So, what brings you two to Whole Foods today?"

"We came to get a bottle of wine and some hummus for our feminist book club," responded Anna with as much friendliness as she could muster.

"Pffft. Why didn't you just make the hummus yourself?" questioned Melissa, arching one of her perfectly-shaped red eyebrows.

"Oh, I was meaning to, but you know, debate tryouts went longer than expected," Anna lied. She had never made hummus in her life, and would never have attempted to do so, even if she had finished work on time She could barely make hard-boiled eggs.

Unfortunately, Melissa was not done with her line of questioning. "So what sort of books does one read at a feminist book club?"

"Well," offered Carlos. "Last month we read Caitlin Moran's memoir *How To Be a Woman* and this month we are discussing Tina Fey's *Bossypants*. We're all super excited for this one."

"Ah," said Melissa casually. "When you said feminist book club, I thought you discussed authors like Simone De Beauvoir, but I am sure that Tina Fey is very good too." Then, without actually looking at her watch or her phone, Melissa added, "Oh no, look at the time! I had better be going home. I am making duck confit for Rajeev tonight. It is our six month anniversary!" Anna detected a smug look in Melissa's eyes.

"Really? I didn't think Rajeev liked duck," replied Anna without thinking.

Detecting something off, Melissa immediately pounced. "How funny! How would you know if Rajeev likes duck?"

"Oh, um, well, I think he mentioned it once, back when he was my student teacher. You know, ages ago." Anna was mortified. She knew she'd aroused Melissa's suspicions.

"You have an unusually good memory then. I can't remember the names of half the teachers I had in high school, let alone their culinary preferences. Still, you should rest assured that Rajeev likes duck when I make it for him. Have a good night!"

Melissa turned on her glossy black patent leather heels and walked away.

When Melissa was safely out of earshot, Carlos turned to his old friend and said bluntly, "Wow, that chick does not like you."

Anna laughed nervously. "Yeah, I'm starting to think that too."

"Starting to think it?" Carlos was incredulous. "Anna, she clearly hates you more than Jennifer Aniston hates Angelina Jolie!"

"Are you drawing comparisons between me and Angelina Jolie?"

"You're right, it was a bad analogy." Carlos smiled at his best friend playfully as he said this.

"Hey!" cried Anna as she punched Carlos in the arm. "Let's go pay for this dip and get over to book club. We wouldn't want to miss all the high-spirited discussion of *Bossypants*." With that, the two friends headed for the checkout line.

It was ten-thirty p.m. and Allie had been holed up in her room feeling miserable for most of the night. She could think of nothing else besides Jack pulling rank, forcing her and Octavia together as debate partners.

Allie rarely gave herself time to sulk. She usually felt there was far too much to do in life to waste her precious time on ruminating. Instead, Allie preferred to bottle up all her feelings, keep calm, and carry on. Tonight, however, all Allie Denning could do was hide away from the world watching old episodes of *New Girl*.

When Allie arrived home earlier that night, Sybilla had chided her daughter for the telltale red eyes that made it obvious she had been crying.

After a few minutes of Allie sitting listlessly at the kitchen island, Sybilla had had enough. "I am not one of those mothers who sees a sulking teenager and wants to comfort her. If you are going to be silent and unsociable, please go upstairs and leave us in peace."

"Sybilla," pleaded Allie's father, who had just arrived home from a business trip to D.C. not an hour before. "I am sure Allie does not mean to be rude. I have missed you both a great deal over the last few days. Let's try to have a pleasant night as a family, okay?"

"That's easy for you to say! While you were off arguing in front of the Supreme Court, and staying at the Mandarin Oriental, I was here, balancing work and raising your daughter!" Sybilla was spurred on by her righteous indignation. "You don't deal with Allie on a daily basis. I'm here more and I know what that girl needs. She doesn't need to be coddled," declared Sybilla with confidence.

"I'm not suggesting we baby Allie. I just don't think we should punish her for having emotions. I mean, have you even asked Allie what's wrong?"

Allie hated it when her parents discussed her as if she were not in the room. For some reason Allie could not understand, her parents frequently argued about how to raise her in front of her. But Allie knew her parents loved each other a great deal. When they weren't butting heads over their conflicting parenting strategies, they held hands and beamed at each other like a couple of teenagers at prom.

Allie's parents had identical views on the importance of the social safety net, the unethical nature of U.S. drone strikes in foreign countries, and the absolute necessity of continuing the fight to achieve pay equity for women. They both loved Chinese food, listening to old Sarah McLachlan albums, and playing Trivial Pursuit. They even watched *Veep* with each other every Sunday night like clockwork, as though it were a sacred ritual. Sybilla and Charles were a great couple, and everyone knew it. They just didn't seem to be compatible co-parents.

While her mom and dad argued over how to parent her, Allie grabbed her schoolbag and went upstairs. She was fairly certain it would be a few minutes before her parents even registered that she was gone.

Now, safely ensconced in her room, Allie felt so lonely that only one person she knew could comfort her. Fortunately, Grandma Trudy, even in her eighties, was still a night owl who could be counted upon to give wise counsel well into the evening. Allie picked up her iPhone and dialled. Trudy Denning answered straight away.

"Hi, Grandma!"

"Hi, my love. How are you tonight?" Her voice sounded bright as ever. Grandma Trudy was the most unfailingly pleasant person in Allie's life.

"I'm sad. Jack is forcing me to debate with this new girl. I barely even know her and she has absolutely no experience!" Allie began to weep all over again.

"Now why would Jack do something like that?" asked Trudy, sounding puzzled.

"Well, he claims to believe this girl has raw talent. He says we can train her, that we can turn her into a great debate partner for me. But ... she's such a *bad* girl, Grandma. Part of me is afraid she won't put in the work, that I'll be stuck with dead weight I can't pull." Allie hesitated for a moment. "But then another part of me is worried she has something I don't. She's such a compelling speaker. I'm worried I don't have that kind of charm." It was a relief to get these insecurities off her chest.

"Now, you listen to me. Bad girls may try, but they can never defeat you. Do you think Jackie Kennedy was happy when that trollop Marilyn Monroe clung to her husband like cheap cologne? Of course she wasn't, but she wasn't beaten by it. Do you know why? Because, at the end of the day, girls like Marilyn get to make a show of themselves singing 'Happy Birthday,' but girls like Jackie get to be First Lady."

"Oh, Grandma, you always bring up Jackie Kennedy whenever you're giving me advice." Allie laughed. While she didn't exactly agree with her grandmother's slut-shaming perspective, it was the first time she had smiled since Jack had paired her with Octavia earlier that day.

"I bring up Jackie Kennedy because I know you are the same type of girl as she was. Jackie was always dignified. No matter who betrayed her, or how unhappy she was on the inside, Jackie never let it show, and that's why Jackie always won." Trudy spoke matter-of-factly. She believed every word she said.

"Allie, Not everyone in this world is lucky enough to have been taught the right way to behave. One isn't born a proper young woman, one becomes one with careful training. You, my darling, are lucky enough to have descended from a long line of Boston Brahmins." Trudy told her granddaughter this in a decidedly triumphant tone.

"Don't forget, my mom is a Lebanese immigrant who grew up in Detroit," Allie reminded her grandmother.

"That may be true, but I know you and you are a Denning through and through." Allie was not sure this was true. She had inherited her mother's hazel eyes, not the signature blue ones the Denning family was famous for in Boston high society. And try as she might, Allie didn't really like to play tennis or golf all that much. Not only that, but she was pretty suspicious of the Country Club for admitting so few members of colour. Even the term "Boston Brahmin," while favoured by Trudy, was something Allie knew to be inexcusably racist.

Still, despite all of her misgivings, Grandma Trudy was the woman who comforted Allie when she had a bad day. Whereas nothing Allie did ever seemed to meet Sybilla's lofty standards, Grandma Trudy was a constant source of approval and praise. In Allie's eyes, the difference between Sybilla and Trudy was that Trudy accepted Allie, even if she insisted on believing Allie was someone she wasn't in order to do so.

"I *am* Jacqueline Kennedy Onassis, I *am* Jacqueline Kennedy Onassis. I *am* Jacqueline Kennedy Onassis," Allie chanted to herself as she got ready for school that Monday morning. She said those words while putting on her uniform, while packing her backpack, while putting her hair into its signature ponytail.

Allie was determined to repeat her new mantra until she felt it with every fibre of her being. Finally, after about an hour of straight repetition, she was starting to believe it.

By the time Allie arrived at the ABC locker room, she was feeling pretty confident in her ability to take the high road with grace and ease. She even waited by Octavia's locker for her to arrive so she could inform Octavia in person of the auspicious news: she would now be a member of the ABC debate team, and partners with its captain.

Octavia eventually arrived about two minutes before the school bell rang. Allie thought this was cutting it a little close, but she tried not to be judgmental. This was her new debate partner after all, and Allie felt the bond between debate partners to be a sacred one.

When Octavia spotted Allie waiting for her as she entered the locker room, she was half convinced Allie was going to shiv her. That girl was simply too perfect. Octavia was certain there had to be a dark side under the polished exterior. Octavia approached warily, but she was undeniably curious about what was going to go down.

"Good morning!" said Allie brightly.

How could anyone be so cheerful at eight-thirteen a.m.?

"Hi, Allie. Um, could you please excuse me? I need to get into my locker." Allie dutifully moved out of the way as Octavia began to fiddle with her lock.

"So, you may be wondering why I'm here, waiting for you?" Allie gave Octavia what was definitely a meaningful look, but Octavia was unsure of what it meant exactly. Allie did not appear to notice Octavia's puzzlement.

"You have probably surmised that I have some big news to share, because you know I am not a stalker!" continued Allie with a laugh. The thing was, Octavia was not so sure Allie wasn't a stalker. No one could be on her best behaviour all of the time. She was sure Allie had some secret vice, and maybe stalking random people was it.

Allie inhaled sharply. "So, I have some information that I believe will make you very happy,"

"Is the cafeteria finally going to start serving mayo, or do I need to resolve myself to a life of veganese?" asked Octavia sarcastically.

"Um, *no*." Allie said, remembering suddenly that she was almost out of Earth Balance. "You made the ABC Debate Team!" Allie continued, giving a little scream of excitement that sounded forced.

"Okay," said Octavia casually, as she opened her locker and began searching for her American history textbook. It would have been more interesting had Allie confessed something like a secret life as a pyromaniac. Octavia had been pretty confident she was going to make the debate team after her showing at tryouts.

"There is more good news," continued Allie in an insincerely cheerful tone. "We are going to be debate partners! Exciting, right? Yay!" Allie had contorted her face into a large grin that seemed about as natural as Bella Hadid wearing flat shoes to a nightclub.

"Oh," replied Octavia coolly, as she zipped her backpack and prepared to leave.

"Oh? That's all you have to say? Making the ABC Debate Team is an honour. Do you know how many girls tried out and didn't make it? Not only that, but you're new to debating and I'm a veteran, but you're still going to be my partner. Starting out with someone experienced by your side is a huge advantage. Almost no one ever gets that. Why aren't you happier about this?" Allie's cheeks were red. She was angry now.

"I haven't decided one hundred percent yet whether or not debating is for me," explained Octavia rather earnestly. In truth, while she had loved speaking in front of everyone at the tryout, Octavia wasn't sure she could spend so much of her time with perfect girls like Allie. She knew for a fact that Imogene would judge her for choosing to do so. Given that Imogene was the only girl Octavia had befriended in the entirety of Boston, that was a definite concern, one that could overshadow the thrill she got from public speaking. After a night of thinking it over, Octavia was still half-convinced Imogene might have been right – maybe debating just wasn't for girls like her.

"What? Why would you waste our time trying out if you didn't even want it?" For a second, Octavia thought Allie was going to huff off, but she did not yet know the girl's tendency to pontificate.

Allie continued, "Also, *who* doesn't want to be on one of the most prestigious high school debate teams in the state? Do you know how impressive debating looks on an application to an Ivy League School?" Octavia didn't but she sensed Allie was about to tell to her. "Excelling at debate can be the difference between going to Brandeis and going to Princeton," spat Allie. Her body was practically shaking with rage. How dare Octavia be so ungrateful? Octavia had been handed an extraordinary opportunity, and here she was acting as if the ABC Debate Team was not good enough for her. Who did Octavia think she was?

"Wow, calm down!" Octavia told Allie. Octavia was half convinced this was the moment when Allie would finally go postal. Though part of her was a bit frightened of what Allie was capable of doing in the tenth grade locker room, another part of Octavia was secretly wishing for the rant to continue. Seeing the completely frantic side of Allie was intriguing.

"Calm down? Did you really just tell me to 'calm down?'" Allie threw her hands up in the air in frustration. "Do you think I wanted to get partnered with you? I had a great debate partner who worked hard and followed all the rules. And then you show up at school with your distressed Rag and Bone boots and your beautifully unkempt curls and suddenly, even though you clearly do not take any pride at all in your academic career, you make it onto the most elite extra-curricular at ABC!"

By this point, a crowd of students had stopped what they were doing to stare at the altercation. Everyone was intrigued by the image of perfect Allie Denning completely losing her cool.

"Not only do you get to be on the debate team, but you get to debate with me, and not to be conceited or anything, but I'm a catch! I was the top-ranked ninth grade debater in the state of Massachusetts last year. So no, some random upstart from Montreal who has never debated a day in her life is not the partner I would have chosen for myself, but I got used to the idea because I thought everyone deserves a chance, even girls who wear black nail polish to school when it is explicitly prohibited in the Code of Conduct."

Allie paused to catch her breath. The bell was about to ring any second now, but Allie wasn't quite done.

"I rose above everything. I rose above my feelings of discomfort regarding debating with you, so why can't you do the same? I am Jackie; you are Marilyn! You should be grateful ABC is giving you this chance to do what so many well behaved young women who actually do wear the uniform properly would love to do!" After her rant was finally over, Allie's mouth was dry and her cheeks and neck were red and spotty. She was brimming with a palpable rage, but in that moment, even though most people would have considered such an outburst inappropriate, Octavia decided she liked Allie more than ever.

"Allie, I was leaning towards yes. I just hadn't completely made up my mind yet. But now that I see it means so much to you, I accept. Just please go splash some cold water on your face before first period. Your face is the colour of a tomato right now." With that, Octavia picked up her backpack, turned on her heel, and walked away.

Over a lunch of gluten-free organic burritos in the cafeteria that afternoon, Imogene confronted Octavia about her plans to join the debate team.

"So, I hear you're going to be one of THOSE girls now?" Imogene said pointedly. They both knew to what she was referring.

"I'm just doing an extra-curricular." Octavia punctuated her statement with a shrug. "Nothing about me is going to change."

"Oh please, debating is a gateway academic drug. In no time you'll be staying in on a Saturday night to write your civics essay instead of crashing keg parties at Boston College with me" Imogen said, lightly touching Octavia's shoulder.

Octavia felt stubborn. "Just because I made the team doesn't mean I'm serious about it. I have no choice. Ms. Knole would make me do it even if I said no." Imogene rolled her eyes, decidedly unimpressed with this excuse. Octavia's mind began racing. It really did look as if Imogene were seriously prepared to walk away from their fledgling friendship if she showed any signs of becoming an involved student. In an effort to appease her, Octavia blurted out, "Hey, think about how annoyed Allie will be to have a partner who doesn't care?"

This made Imogene smile. "Okay, I admit this could be an interesting social experiment."

Octavia was relieved. Imogene was the only girl she'd met in Boston who seemed to know where to get a fake ID, and which liquor stores would pretend to believe they were real. The daughter of former Olympic equestrians who started their own wildly successful line of athletic clothes called Brookline Active Wear, Imogene had tons of money and very little parental supervision. Her parents spent most of their time toiling at their company's headquarters in downtown Boston, or visiting their manufacturers' in Taiwan. In light of this, Imogene had both the means and the opportunity to do whatever she pleased.

"So, are we still going to visit that bar you told me about this weekend? The one in Cambridge?" Octavia ventured hopefully.

"Oh totes. Just tell the dons in the boarding house that you're sleeping over at my place. I mean, it's not even necessarily a lie. At some point, after we get our drink on, we might go home and do some sleeping."

Octavia considered what this night might entail. She was slowly beginning to understand that this was a sink or swim situation for her: accept this friendship with Imogene, or risk being relegated to the debate team's social circle, if they would even accept her, or worse, be a total loner.

Octavia grinned at Imogene. "I'm so in."

7.

IGNORANCE ISN'T BLISS
WHEN YOU'RE A DEBATER

ALLIE AND OCTAVIA were at their first debating practice as partners. Seated in the school's library, they were meant to be doing research for the Howard Cup, an annual debate tournament held in the first week of October at Hillsview Preparatory School. The Howard Cup was named for the school's first headmaster, a colonial era gentleman by the name of George Isaiah Howard. Dying with no heirs, Headmaster Howard left all of his worldly possessions to Hillsview, and in honour of the man who paid for a wing of classrooms that burned down in a fluke fire in 1921, Hillsview still hosted a debating tournament in his name.

The topic of debate was announced a month before the tournament and was always on an international political issue, in an attempt to force the participants to expand their horizons. Research wasn't just an asset, it was a necessity. Students sometimes showed up with entire duffle bags full of newspaper articles and academic journals, ready to pounce on their opponents with more facts than an Almanac.

"Okay," said Allie. "Let's get to work. The resolution we are researching for the debate is the following: Be It Resolved that Turkey should be part of the European Union. It's an interesting one, don't you think, Octavia?"

"Okay, Allie. This debate is in three weeks. Don't you think it's a little overkill to start thinking about it now?" asked Octavia, slouching in her seat.

"We're actually running a bit behind schedule. The resolution was announced a couple of weeks ago now. The tournament's winners usually understand the issues backwards and forewords, so we have to make up for lost time Do you have any prior knowledge of this subject?" Allie asked in a business-like tone.

"Um, well, I know the EU is that organization of European countries where Germany pays for everything." While flippant and not entirely fair, Octavia's answer was definitely more accurate than Allie had anticipated.

"Okay, that's a bit reductive, but not entirely wrong," conceded Allie. "So what do you know about Turkey?"

Octavia did not know much about Turkey at all. She rarely read the newspaper. Reading the newspaper was something responsible people did, and as someone who had never, even on her best day, been called responsible, Octavia felt she was exempted from this social convention.

Allie began to look impatient for an answer, so Octavia decided to get it over with. "Okay, so here's what I know about Turkey: they make great kebabs there and Istanbul has an up and coming fashion week."

"Do you know anything about their history of military coups? Or their government's laws that restrict freedom of speech? Do you know what Turkey's economy is based on? Do you know the name of their prime minister? Do you ... do you even know where Turkey IS?" Allie fired off these questions in a pointed tone. She was desperate to prove to Octavia that there was a reason ABC girls prepared for these tournaments in advance.

Of course, Octavia seemed smart. Allie admitted this to herself. But it was also fairly obvious that Octavia was not as knowledgeable about the world as a successful debater should be. Allie knew this had to change or their partnership would be doomed.

Octavia, however, felt incredibly frustrated with Allie. Surely there was no need to panic. How hard could kids at the other schools seriously be working to prepare for this debate?

"Look, I don't know that stuff., But I doubt it will be necessary to know so much detail. I know the basics, so if worse comes to worse, I can just wing it," asserted Octavia while reaching into her blazer for her iPhone to check the time. It was four-fifteen p.m. already, an entire forty-five minutes after the last class had finished. How long after school did Allie expect Octavia to stay, exactly?

Octavia was getting antsy. She was over being at practice and absolutely desperate to FaceTime Marcus. Octavia had to call him soon, or she'd miss him. She knew he was planning to attend a concert that night with his friends.

Allie gave Octavia a meaningful look of irritation. After a dramatic pause for effect, she asked point blank, "Octavia, do you even know what language they speak in Turkey?"

Without missing a beat, Octavia replied, "Duh! Arabic."

"Oh my God, they speak TURKISH in TURKEY!" shouted Allie so loudly a bunch of other girls in the library stopped their typing to turn and stare. Allie was too annoyed to notice all the gaping mouths.

"Do you think you're better than me just because you know these things? So I have a life. So I prefer to go out with friends instead of staying home reading *The Economist* and watching MSNBC like some sort of news-obsessed shut-in. That doesn't make me stupid."

"No, you're not stupid at all, Octavia. But do you know what they call smart people who choose not to know anything about the world? They call them ignorant," spat Allie with a hostility that surprised even her.

Octavia flushed with rage. She was usually so nonplussed about everything. Yet Allie had somehow managed to puncture her laid-back exterior. How dare she call her ignorant? The self-righteous Allie Denning didn't know her. Octavia was certain that just because she wasn't an over-achiever, that did not make her ignorant. Octavia tried to convince herself that Allie was just a freak, a girl who spent her evenings reading foreign policy weeklies instead of texting a boyfriend or trying to sneak a joint. Normal girls spent more time listening to Kanye West than NPR's Democracy Now. So where did Allie get off judging her? Perhaps Imogene had been right, Octavia thought to herself. Maybe debating was just too brainy and intense for her liking.

Octavia gathered her things. She could not be in the same room as someone who had just offended her so profoundly. "I'm out of here," she announced. "I refuse to be lectured by someone like you. The closest you've ever gotten to making out with a guy is fantasizing about Jon Stewart!"

Octavia actually did not know this for certain. She barely knew Allie at all. Octavia was also aware that it wasn't really that creative an insult, but she was fairly certain it would be offensive enough to make an impression on Allie, so Octavia decided to exit the room on this note. Allie stayed behind, looking embarrassed as the other girls in the room giggled over Octavia's dig at her level of intimate physical experience.

For a few moments, Allie was too stunned to continue working. Was it so obvious she had never been kissed? Allie was not particularly ashamed of this fact. She was not exactly boy crazy. She found most young men her age to be tiresome and juvenile. The ones she met through debating were some-what more interesting, but they were her competitors, so she avoided socializing with them too much. After all, who wants to humanize an opponent?

Still, the idea that everyone KNEW she had yet to be kissed made Allie slightly uncomfortable. How did anyone other than Lainey and Bailey know she had virgin lips? What about her made it so obvious? Was she simply the world's least attractive human being? Was it apparent to all who beheld her that it would be impossible for Allie Denning ever to have a suitor?

Allie blinked back tears. Perhaps she was completely unkiss-able. Perhaps she would never ever know anything other than platonic embraces from boys she liked. Perhaps Octavia, with her relaxed attitude and effortless, laid-back beauty would get to canoodle with all the boys she wanted in life, but Allie was certain she had one thing over Octavia: her unwavering work ethic. Allie went back to googling facts about Turkey. After all, her personal life motto was "Keep Calm and Carry On."

Anna was just about to go home for the night when she heard someone knocking aggressively at her door.

"Come in," Anna called, feeling a bit nervous about who might appear, and what they might want. Anna was supposed to be meeting up with some friends from grad school at a pub in Cambridge that evening. She had been looking forward to seeing their reassuring faces all week, and she definitely did not want to be late. The weekend had finally arrived and Anna wanted a glass of red wine. As a teacher, wasn't this Friday night libation her God-given right?

Anna's door opened to reveal none other than Octavia Irving. Octavia, with her history of spotty grades and her fondness for violating rules about the uniform, was what most people would have referred to as a "problem student." Anna, however, saw potential.

Octavia was smart. She was analytical and well spoken, but unfortunately for everyone who tried to teach her, Octavia also did not seem to care much about anything other people told her was important. It almost seemed to be on principle that Octavia Irving hated all things adults tried to convince her were priorities. Still, Anna believed if she could just find a way to deal with the girl's attitude problem, Octavia could become almost anything she wanted to be.

"I don't want to do debating anymore," gasped Octavia before she'd even closed the door. Anna was surprised to see her normally insouciant student blinking back tears.

Anna motioned for Octavia to sit down. "What happened?"

"Allie is too intense for me. She's mad at me for not knowing anything about Turkey. Why does she care? It's my life! If I don't care about foreign politics, who is she to judge me for it?" spat a fuming Octavia.

Anna thought for a second about how to respond. She did not want to alienate Octavia, and yet she suspected Allie might not have been completely in the wrong. Of course, Anna assumed Allie had probably said something uncalled for in the heat of the moment. At the same time, Octavia was Allie's partner, so of course she had every right to care if Octavia knew about Turkey. This was especially true when the two of them would have to debate together on whether the country should be admitted to the EU.

"Octavia, you're right that Allie should not judge you so harshly. It's not nice to feel judged like that."

Octavia gave a half-smile in response, thinking Anna's words meant she had gotten the guidance counsellor firmly on her side.

"Having said that, debating is a competitive activity and it's done in pairs. If you choose not to hand in a history assignment, you are only screwing yourself over, but if you don't do the work here, you're screwing Allie over too. Is that fair?"

Octavia desperately did not want to concede that Ms. Knole might have a point, so she said nothing at all.

"Octavia, why don't you want to do the research for this debate? Do you find it boring?"

"No," admitted Octavia. The few facts she had gleaned in the prep session with Allie admittedly were pretty fascinating. Octavia had no idea there were so many military coups (and coup attempts) in recent Turkish history. She was curious about how those all played out.

"Okay then, so did you have somewhere else you urgently needed to be?" continued Anna.

Octavia decided not to mention Marcus. Instead, she conceded, "Not really. I have at most one friend in Boston. It's an exceptional day when I have a social engagement. Plus, I'm not an old lady with blue hair who lives in West Palm Beach, so my parties don't usually start in the late afternoon."

"Well, then, why didn't you want to do research for the debate this afternoon?" Anna felt on the verge of a breakthrough.

"I don't know," answered Octavia. It was an honest answer. Truth be told, she knew Marcus likely would have been too busy to talk to her even if she had called. He had been blowing their phone calls off a lot lately. He had never really been a fan of in-person calls, preferring to send Octavia Snapchats from bars or from his Crossfit classes.

Anna took a deep breath before speaking again. "Octavia, do you think sometimes you sabotage yourself because you're secretly afraid that, even if you try your best, you won't be good enough?"

Octavia was stunned. What was there to say in response? Was that true? She honestly didn't know. Of course, Octavia knew her father would be pleased if she could be the kind of kid who did well in school and excelled at extra-curricular pursuits, like his sons with Shira. He liked bragging about his kids. Shira's strict parenting style also ensured Octavia's younger brothers had a lot to brag about. They were classical violinists who were always at the top of their classes at Toronto's Upper Canada College. Octavia knew her father. When he could be bothered, he probably compared her younger half-brothers to her. Octavia also knew the comparisons were likely not so favourable, as she was the family's far less accomplished offspring.

Neither Mordecai nor Octavia's free spirit mother ever seemed to put much effort into motivating her to be anything other than a disappointment. She couldn't remember the last time she'd been chided for a poor grade or encouraged to try just a little bit harder at tennis.

Octavia had always assumed her lack of effort at the things adults valued was something she couldn't help. Her apathy had been there for so long, it seemed inevitable. Octavia had always assumed it was a natural aspect of her being until meeting Ms. Knole. Suddenly, however, her indifference to school no longer seemed like so much of a given. Still, she wasn't necessarily prepared to admit that.

Octavia eventually broke the silence saying, "I don't know if my distaste for the excessive debating research sessions required by Allie Denning means I have a secret fear of failure."

"You're right," responded Anna in an even tone. "I could just be over-analyzing everything. Even so, I want you to know that you really shouldn't be afraid of failing. I have a feeling that if you worked harder, you could totally win that debate tournament."

"I don't think I have what Allie has," blurted out Octavia unexpectedly, surprising even herself. "She knows things and she gets what they mean. She's always going on about the different kinds of secularism and the differences between political parties in countries I've never even thought about. I don't know if I can learn all that."

"Well, I know you can," Anna told her student with the utmost confidence.

Octavia sat for a moment, speechless. No one had ever had such an unwavering belief in her abilities before. Anna's faith in Octavia was purely contagious, making Octavia herself think that perhaps she could accomplish great things. It was an intoxicating feeling, this sense of possibility. Octavia felt like she had just come in from a long, cold night to have a kind soul wrap her in a layer of cosy blankets, and seat her by a roaring fireplace. For the first time in a long time, Octavia Irving felt like going home and doing some work.

Octavia left Ms. Knole's office that night and went back to her room in the ABC boarding halls. In no time, she was googling various facts about Turkey and the EU. She even cancelled her plans with Imogene to keep working, texting Imogene that she had to bail because of menstrual cramps. Octavia only stopped her research when it was time for bed.

8.

PRETTY IN PUKE

THE AFFAIR WAS a spectacle to behold. It was Bailey Holbeck's sixteenth birthday party, and as far as William and Babe Holbeck were concerned, only the best would do for their daughter. At first, Bailey had wanted her party to be held at The Liberty, a posh, modern hotel downtown. It had once been a prison. For Grandmother Nan, however, this was absolutely out of the question.

"William!" she barked at her son, "It simply won't do. What will the Jennings say? And the Manns? I doubt they would even come to a party in a glorified jail cell! We must have it at the Club."

Bailey, however, had no intention of holding her sweet sixteen at the Country Club. She whined that every single event was held there, and that her birthday party needed to have a certain "It Factor" that made it more special than a Taylor Swift concert. After weeks of deliberation, the family finally settled on the tearoom at the storied Langham Place Hotel. Bailey was happy that at least her birthday would be held downtown, and her grandmother was happy it would be held in a place the Boston Strangler had never called home.

William and Babe were so pleased with this arrangement, that they planned a further surprise for Bailey. Savannah, their eldest daughter, had suggested her mom and dad rent the hotel's adjoining presidential suites for the evening. Bailey and her ABC friends would stay in one room, while Savannah would quietly chaperone from the adjoining suite, originally meant for the president's security detail.

What William and Babe were unaware of was that the surprise of gifting the girls the suite for the evening would in fact be no surprise at all to Bailey. The sisters had always been close. They were fierce competitors yes, but they were cut from the same cloth (Grandmother Nan's, of course). They understood each other implicitly, were avid students of Game Theory, and when a plan could be formulated that would benefit them both, they were quite frankly unstoppable.

Savannah had been planting the idea in her parents' minds that renting the suite would be the most fabulous gift for Bailey's birthday. She had finally told Bailey of the plan when their parents had agreed to it and informed Savannah so she could plan to spend the night at the Langham with her sister and her sister's friends. Bailey was overjoyed with the news. Savannah told her simply to "stay out of her way for the night" as she was planning on inviting her own friends to party in her suite, and of course her boyfriend would spend the night. And so, the sisters agreed to enjoy the fruits of Savannah's labour, and to give one another their space.

William and Babe weren't complete idiots, of course. They realized their daughters might get themselves into some she-nanigans on their own in a couple of hotel rooms. In their minds, however, the most that could possibly go wrong was that the girls might swipe a small bottle of rum from the mini bar. While such an occurrence wouldn't be ideal, they thought it better for their daughters to rebel in a five-star hotel than in some seedy bar near Boston College.

What sealed their decision was the sweet sixteen birthday party their friends', the Manns, had thrown for their daughter, Daisy. Held in Charleston, South Carolina, where the Manns kept their ancestral family home, the party had been more extravagant than the most extravagant of Southern society weddings, let alone teenage girls' birthday parties.

It goes without saying that the affair was black tie. Several tents were set up around the storied property, a former cotton plantation with a horrific history of slavery that everyone seemed to forget about as soon as the wine was poured and crab cakes were served. One tent was meant strictly for the adults attending the party. Dinner had been flown in from a Daniel Boulud restaurant in New York, but the highlight was when the guests regaled themselves with a snack of barbecue and champagne at midnight. It was such a "novel!" event several drunken parents exclaimed as they stumbled out of the party and into their chauffeured cars at the end of the evening.

The Mann family had created a new standard in Southern hospitality. Babe Holbeck may have moved to Boston after meeting her husband at the Republican National Convention in 1996, but her heart was still invested in being the best high society belle she could be.

Unfortunately, even though the Holbecks' bank accounts were fat by the standards of those not in the top one percent of earners, they didn't compare to the mammoth wealth of the Manns, who had made hundreds of millions from oil and gas. It was impossible to out-do them where spending was concerned, but if the Holbecks could offer their daughter something Daisy's parents hadn't thought to give her, there was a chance they could win this round of competitive party planning.

The idea that Daisy had likely complained to her parents about how she spent her sweet sixteen birthday night in her childhood bedroom, coupled with the fact that she would be excluded from the sleepover at the Langham – as it would be an "ABC girls only sleepover, I'm sure you understand" — was too delicious for the Holbecks to ignore. And so, they agreed with Savannah and rented out the presidential suites. Potential for naughty teenage antics be damned!

To show off their generosity to all other parents at school, Bailey was forced to invite each and every ABC student in her grade. This even included the ones she worried might outshine her, like Octavia. Octavia, with her hipster taste in music and gorgeous head of hair, was just the type of girl Bailey knew her on-off boyfriend Austin would love. It caused Bailey great distress to think that they would be at the same fete tonight of all nights, when it was supposed to be *her night*.

For her part, Octavia had considered not going at all. In fact, Bailey had only mentioned the party to her at debate practice the day before, right before Octavia's run in with Allie over researching Turkey. At the time, Octavia suspected Bailey had extended the invitation more so she could show off by inviting as many people as possible than as a true overture of friendship. Octavia didn't know Bailey beyond their brief interactions in class and at debate practice, where Bailey had barely spoken more than five words to her. Because of this, the thought of spending an entire night with her seemed awkward, but in the end, Imogene had convinced Octavia to go. "I don't like Bailey, either," Imogene had laughed. "But there won't be any parents there, so when the Hillsview boys show up, it'll turn into a rager." Ultimately Octavia decided it would be better to spend the night at a fancy hotel instead of the ABC dorm, even if it was at the birthday party of someone whose primary interactions with her had been insulting sneers.

At approximately ten-thirty p.m., Bailey's parents decided the party had gone perfectly, and had been very well attended. Giddy with victory, Babe and William Holbeck piled into their Land Rover to return home to Beacon Hill. They had gotten the girls settled into the suite upstairs, and were satisfied with the delight they had witnessed (throwing pillows, jumping on beds, helping themselves to the heaping jars of candy the hotel had dutifully set up). Gratified the plan was a hit, Bailey's parents took a few photos with their iPhones to capture the moment for posterity on Instagram, and left.

The moment the adults departed, of course, the girls took the opportunity to change out of their party frocks and into more form-fitting clothes. Bailey put on Beyoncé's "Drunk In Love" to set the tone. She did, however, make sure to keep it down, as it was far too early to get hotel security scuttling up to interfere with their party.

The girls had finished fixing each other's hair and make up when there was a knock at the door. Bailey smoothed her Rebecca Taylor strapless dress and went to answer it. She hoped it would be her boyfriend, Austin, there to greet her with a sensual birthday kiss. What she found, however, was even more exciting to her than the sight of her clean-cut Lacrosse player boyfriend.

"Ladies…" Teddy purred as he sauntered in holding a bright orange bag packed with chilled bottles of champagne."

Teddy!" Bailey squealed, "You shouldn't have! How did you manage this?"

"I have my ways," Teddy haughtily replied as he surveyed the room.

Teddy St. Germaine was a playboy of epic proportions and as such, was a fixture on the prep school party scene. There were rumours Teddy had lost his virginity to his Spanish teacher at Hillsview at the beginning of ninth grade. Now, two years after that, Teddy was said to have bedded at least twenty other women, including an Israeli flight attendant, the hottest waitress at the Copley Centre Legal Seafood, a Kennedy, and, perhaps less probably, Kendall Jenner. Teddy had made a career of hooking up with beautiful, glamorous women. He was always looking for his next torrid encounter.

Soon after his arrival, Teddy clocked Octavia. He gazed at her hopefully with his seductive bedroom eyes; however, she returned his lustful glances with an unimpressed smirk. She then continued to reapply her lipstick. Teddy decided to move on to other romantic candidates.

Teddy's eyes next fell on Lainey, who was sitting on the edge of the bed. Her black hair was let loose, swishing back and forth neatly as she turned to look around the room. For the first time, he also noticed her cherubic lips. He was undeniably intrigued.

Teddy was primed to make his advances on Lainey when he was interrupted by the arrival of a large group of fellow students from Hillsview. They ran in like a football team, one of them practically body-checking Teddy in his excitement to be at a party with no adults in sight.

And with that, the real party was in full swing. The fact all the teens assembled had previously seen each other at Bailey's dinner earlier that night only increased the boys' excitement at seeing the girls again. This time, the kids could ogle each other to their hearts' content without the judgmental stares of their parents following their every move. This time, no one had to be on their best behaviour, and everyone could do exactly what they wanted.

Imogene arrived at the same time as the boys. She looked stunning in a daring black slip dress and her signature Frye boots. She had stepped out for a liquor run of her own, lying to Bailey's parents that she needed to go home urgently because her elderly cat, Razzles, had just died. Little did they know that Imogene had never had a pet cat in her life.

Imogene's face was free of makeup, and her hair was pulled back into a low, messy bun, blonde tendrils framing her delicate features. She immediately pulled up a chair next to Octavia and whispered to her that she had brought some "party favours," and with that the two girls went off to smoke a joint on the balcony. They had no interest in drinking fruity coolers with the less experienced people at the party.

Octavia and Imogene stepped into the warm and breezy night, settling into the sofa on the balcony. As Imogene expertly lit the joint in one fluid motion, she glanced up and noticed Octavia studying her. Imogene giggled, "I've done this a couple of times, can you tell?"

Octavia laughed too but her heart wasn't in it. She suddenly felt very far from home. The girls passed the joint between themselves several times before Teddy poked his head out onto the balcony. He ran to grab Imogene by the hand, telling her she had to see what was going on inside. He didn't invite Octavia in. After the dirty look she'd given him earlier that night, Teddy was planning to keep his distance from her for the rest of the evening.

So Octavia sat alone for a while. She was actually grateful to have some time to herself. Usually a social butterfly, she was finding a party populated by people she didn't know very well surprisingly difficult to handle. Staring at the brilliantly starry sky the penthouse view afforded her, and huddled under a cosy cashmere throw, Octavia barely noticed the French doors open. A tall body slipped out of the suite discretely. He clearly thought he was alone, as he made his way out to the edge of the balcony, peering over the side, then pushing himself back with his muscular arms. He sighed, clearly deep in thought. Octavia waited, wondering whether to say something, but it was ultimately unnecessary. In the darkness, the boy felt someone watching him, and finally looked her way. Their eyes met, they could feel – if not completely see – each other in the darkness.

"Hi," said Austin after a moment.

"Hi," Octavia breathed, the only response she could muster. After a silence, she elaborated, "Sorry, I should introduce myself. My name's Octavia, I was just trying to get away from everything inside, so are you, I'm guessing. Either that, or thinking suicidal thoughts. Oh wait, no ... I didn't mean that thing about suicidal thoughts. Sorry, that was inappropriately dark humour for someone I've never met." Octavia was babbling, something she couldn't remember having done with anyone before.

Austin laughed easily, and Octavia noticed she felt warm and flushed when he did so. He made his way over to her and asked, "May I sit with you?" She shuffled over, thinking he might sit beside her. Instead, he took up residence in an armchair next to the sofa she was perched on.

"I'm Austin, by the way." He extended his hand.

Octavia extended her own hand back without hesitation. She was now used to the handshaking formality of these Boston prep school kids. Austin's fingers felt soft against her skin. For a moment, she wished their handshake could go on forever. There was a long silence as the two just stared, each taking the other in as fully as they could.

Eventually, Austin broke the silence with some small talk. "So, I hear you're from Montreal?"

"I am," she replied, somewhat taken aback. Octavia's big eyes widened. "How do you know that?"

"Oh, you're pretty much the story of the moment with the Hillsview contingent at this soiree. You've definitely caught the eye of more than one guy here," he said shyly. "I don't want to be creepy, I just thought I should warn you of all the ... *attention* you're about to receive."

Octavia instinctively blurted, "I have a boyfriend. He's in university ... college, I mean. Oh, whatever, you *know* what I mean." She sensed a slight edge of disappointment from Austin, but couldn't be exactly sure.

"That's cool, that's also part of what people are talking about. That you have a boyfriend...." Austin trailed off, much to Octavia's relief. For some reason, she did not want to talk about Marcus with Austin.

"Do you have a girlfriend?" asked Octavia. She sounded shyer than she'd meant to.

"Sort of – I mean, yes, I do. It's Bailey. We've been together for a long time, almost two years now, but uh, I broke up with her during the summer because—" Austin cut off suddenly, as though he couldn't not think of a way to finish that sentence. "Anyway, we got back together last month, right before school started. So yeah, I guess she's my girlfriend. I'm here as her date." The word "date" came off his tongue dryly.

Octavia felt an uncomfortable mixture of shock and disappointment. The shock was obvious, Austin seemed so ...

decent. She could not understand how Austin and Bailey could possibly be coupled together. The disappointment she felt was more perplexing, however. She resolved in that split second to bury it away, and to provide it with no further analysis.

Octavia, betraying none of her true feelings, exclaimed, "Well, I'm happy for you, Bailey's a great girl" Austin nodded in agreement, but with a palpable lack of enthusiasm.

In an instant, the delightful encounter between Octavia and Austin was over. The balcony doors swung open dramatically. A pair of intent blue eyes searched for her errant boyfriend, and she was none too pleased to find him getting cosy with Octavia Irving.

Bailey sauntered over. She crooned sweetly, "Austin, honey, I've been looking everywhere for you. We're just about to play spin the bottle. So funny, right? It's Teddy's idea, of course. Won't you come inside and join me?" Bailey was working strenuously to ignore Octavia's presence. She hadn't made eye contact with her once. Bailey had only agreed to invite Octavia because her parents felt it was necessary to invite her entire grade in an effort to prove to the Mann family they did nothing by halves. Truth be told, she had put off extending the invitation for as long as she possibly could.

"Of course we'll come in," Austin replied, gesturing to Octavia. Bailey felt the emphasis in "we" and her cheeks coloured.

"Oh, that's what I meant," she said. "Both of you, please come join the game!"

"Bailey, we're ready!" a girl named Ella shrieked from inside. In response, Bailey immediately turned her fake smile up a notch, then turned on her very high patent leather black heels, and returned to the adoring crowd gathered there to celebrate her.

Still seated, Octavia looked at Austin quizzically, asking with a glance why he would risk the wrath of Bailey, just so she wouldn't feel left out? As if psychically sensing Octavia's thoughts, he gave a kind smile and shrugged.

Austin got up from his seat. For a moment, he looked up at

the sky, while Octavia looked up at him. He appeared lost in the sublime beauty of Boston's cityscape, illuminated against the night sky. After a few moments, Austin turned back toward Octavia, extended his hand and murmured, "I think it's safe to go in. Shall we?"

A part of Octavia she was trying to ignore hoped to see something grander in his gesture than the niceties of a polite young man. The only things she could see for certain in Austin's eyes, however, were sweetness and friendship. Ignoring another twinge of disappointment, Octavia followed her new acquaintance inside.

Upon crossing the threshold into the room, Austin and Octavia's entrance together raised quite a few eyebrows. Surprisingly, Bailey wasn't among the on-lookers. Rather, she was lying on her stomach laughing uncontrollably on a bed with Madison Gerrard, a second cousin on her father's side who happened to be in eleventh grade at ABC.

Austin dutifully went to join his girlfriend's side, and for a minute, Octavia felt lost. Where would she go now? This feeling, however, would not last long.

"Octavia! Get yourself over here now!" Imogene called out from a circle on the floor in the sitting room, "Come sit, this game of spin the bottle is high-larious," Imogene punctuated her statement with a giggle, acknowledging the cheesiness of a pun she only found funny under the influence of mind-altering substances.

"So happy you've come to join us, Octavia," said a Hillsview Lacrosse star named Josh. He was perched cross-legged on several pillows. He had never met Octavia, but like everyone else assembled at the party, Josh knew exactly who she was.

Octavia smiled with just a hint of sarcasm. She peered around the circle, examining each person she might be subjected to kissing. There was Imogene next to her. She was pretty sure Imogene wouldn't mind kissing another girl if it garnered her admiration from the boys. Next there was Teddy, whom

Octavia thought would probably try to grope anything that moved. Next to Teddy was Josh. Then of course there was Hunter Clark, another Hillsview junior, and lastly there was ... Lainey?

Octavia did a double take. Lainey was someone she couldn't quite figure out. Lainey had a quiet intelligence and an even demeanor; however, Octavia also knew from being in the same English class as Lainey that, when pressed by the teacher, she had very informed and well developed opinions about everything from the portrayal of women in the novels of Charles Dickens, to the poetry of Christina Rossetti, whoever that was.

Octavia respected Lainey for the most part. She didn't seem as judgmental as Allie Denning, and yet, Octavia was surprised Lainey would be interested in "Spin the Bottle." Octavia had long ago written Lainey off as a bit of a bore, socially speaking.

This made Octavia wonder – just for a moment – if perhaps she too pigeonholed people too easily?

By the time Octavia redirected her attention back to the game at hand, it was Hunter's turn to spin. The bottle landed almost immediately on Teddy. "Old school rules!" Teddy cried, referring to the homophobic stipulation that despite "Spin the Bottle" being a game designed to create random lip locks, boys would not be kissing other boys. Of course, he did not believe the same rules should be applied to the girls present.

Hunter spun again. The bottle pointed to Octavia this time.

"Of course," she hissed under her breath as Hunter approached, ready to claim his prize. She wasn't thrilled, but would be the first to admit that Hunter was gorgeous. His mother was a South American supermodel and his father a retired quarterback for the New England Patriots.

Hunter smiled lustfully, pleased with the placement and direction of the bottle's neck; however, he was surprisingly respectful as he gave Octavia the politest of brief pecks on the lips.

For a second, Octavia felt a pang of guilt. She had enjoyed her perfunctory kiss with Hunter despite having a boyfriend back home in Montreal. Of course, she didn't feel attracted to him in the kind of way that confused her to the point of having to repress her feeling for the purposes of survival.

Octavia spun next. The empty green bottle of Moet and Chandon mercifully did a full three-hundred-and-sixty degrees and landed on Octavia herself. In light of this, she happily forfeited her turn. Next, Imogene spun the bottle, which landed squarely on Teddy. Octavia turned to Imogene, wondering how she would feel about this. It was a lucky coincidence, as Imogene had spent hours moaning to Octavia about her unrequited lust for Teddy.

As soon as the bottle stopped moving, Imogene's eyes lit up, and she crawled on all fours to Teddy. When she reached her destination, she confidently planted a long kiss on his mouth that lasted several seconds longer than the rules of the game called for. She ended the kiss by playfully tousling his hair before retreating back to her spot, like a cat post-canary.

Eager for more action, Teddy took his turn to spin with the enthusiasm of a poolside DJ in Miami. The bottle spun once, twice, three times before it finally landed on its intended target. Teddy was quite satisfied to see that the make out Gods were on his side tonight, as the bottle landed on just the girl he wanted: Lainey.

In a flash, he was crawling lustfully toward Lainey on his knees. He was besotted by her dark eyes, the blunted ends of her cute shoulder-length bob. She was nerdier than the girls he usually hooked up with to be sure, but that was part of what he liked about her. While Teddy was not a sparkling student himself, he really respected girls who thought a lot, and Lainey was definitely one of those.

Teddy smiled down at Lainey. In what he hoped would be interpreted as a chivalrous gesture, he offered his hand. Lainey accepted it reluctantly. She knew Teddy was empirically gorgeous. That grin was famous all over Boston for bringing women to their knees – often in a literal fashion in the privacy of Teddy's pool house. Lainey knew almost all the other girls at the party wished they were in her shoes. And if she'd been able to, she certainly would have taken off her heels and given them to someone else who wanted to wear them. Unfortunately, this didn't seem possible.

Soon Teddy was gently grasping Lainey by the waist. He stared deeply into her eyes before leaning in to kiss her. The kiss was a deliberate one. It was crafted with the expertise of a great artist. This was no surprise, as Teddy St. Germaine was something of a Jackson Pollock where making out was concerned. He kissed Lainey firmly, slowly, and with great passion.

After Teddy pulled away from Lainey's mouth gracefully, a stunned Bailey felt the need to remark upon what she had seen. "What *was* that, you guys?" she asked in her trademark sing-song-y voice.

Octavia watched Imogene stare jealously at Teddy and Lainey. Meanwhile, Teddy only had eyes for the newest object of his affections. Lainey, however, seemed much more focused on surveying Imogene's face. Was she worried she may have upset her? Octavia thought this was curious. After all, Imogene was not friends with any of the ABC good girls. Why would Lainey care so much what she thought?

Suddenly, the answer for why Lainey cared so much about what Imogene thought dawned on her. She finally understood the three of them, but she wasn't certain they understood each other, or even themselves.

Not one to be left out of the action for long, Imogene seemed determined to get Teddy's attention. If he was going to stare at Lainey, then the natural strategy, Imogene surmised, was to get closer to Lainey. Much closer. In a physical sense.

Imogene grabbed Lainey by the hand. "You know what these boys assembled here tonight would really like?" Her rhetorical question was a loud and dramatic one.

"Nachos?" asked Lainey. She wasn't trying to be funny. She was a bit tipsy and it really was her best guess.

"I can think of something they'd like even more than nachos. Let's make out. That is, if you're game..." Imogene gave an expectant look.

"Oh, I'm game!" Lainey responded quickly. She went on to qualify her answer, "You know, I think the boys would like it. They'll think it's hot. Let's do it for them! You know, because they'll like it..." Lainey's babbling was finally interrupted by Imogene's mouth on hers.

Imogene spared no energy. She used tongue quite aggressively, pulled at Lainey's hair and caressed her face. Lainey did not know that Imogene kept her eyes open and on Teddy the whole time, just to see if he was noticing them. Since Teddy seemed riveted by the display, Imogene let it go on for a very long time.

When it was all over, Imogene walked away without a word. She was off to pursue Teddy, hoping now that she had proven sexually adventurous, he might be more interested in her.

Lainey, however, was stunned. She felt a bit light-headed. She desperately wanted to find a quiet corner to sit and think, but that was not in store for her. Hillsview's star hockey player, Mitchell Glazier, proved to have a weaker stomach than he thought. After imbibing too much, he dramatically and publically projectile vomited onto the king-sized bed where Bailey herself was holding court.

"Ew!" screamed Bailey. "You ruined my birthday! Now the room is going to stink! I will hate you forever now, Mitchell!"

Bailey erupted into tears and had to be comforted by Lainey and Austin for the rest of the evening. All thoughts of Imogene were pushed to the side.

As Octavia reflected on all the drama at the party when she was back in her room at ABC the next day, it occurred to Octavia that one person was missing from the events in the hotel room. Who was that person? None other than Allie Denning. As one of Bailey's best and oldest friends, surely she wouldn't have missed the slumber party, and yet she hadn't been there for any of it. Not the dancing to Beyonce or the underage drinking, and certainly not the game of Spin the Bottle. How curious!

In reality, what Octavia didn't know was that when no one was looking, Allie snuck off. Being somewhat of an expert at avoiding peer pressure, Allie pro-actively barricaded herself into one of the suite's three luxurious bathrooms, creating her very own fortress of solitude

Allie brought a few throw pillows and a blanket with her, arranging them neatly in the gigantic Jacuzzi tub. Once comfortable, she proceeded to read Hilary Clinton's memoir *Hard Choices* all night long on the kindle she always kept in her purse, in case of emergencies.

Allie was fairly certain her friends would be too wasted to wonder where she was. She wasn't worried at all about missing out on the fun. Allie was fairly certain a hotel room party represented everything she believed was bad in the world.

In fact, Allie viewed it as somewhat of a betrayal that Bailey would throw such a soiree in the first place. She fondly remembered simpler times, when their birthdays had involved tea parties at The Fairmont. Allie felt betrayed by Bailey and Lainey. For they had crossed over to the dark side. All of a sudden, underage drinking was their new thing and crumpets with a pot of Earl Grey were nowhere to be found.

"Everything changed when Octavia showed up," Allie thought to herself when she woke up the next morning. She was lying in an empty bathtub with her kindle resting on her chest. She was sure that Octavia's rebellious ways were somehow contagious, and were infecting all of her previously well-behaved friends.

9.

THE SOCIAL HANGOVER

I T WAS THE DAY AFTER Bailey's sweet sixteen birthday party. Lainey, Bailey, and Allie were studying for their French test in Allie's bedroom. As diligent as these girls were, of their five-hour study session, at least two hours involved more gossiping about the events of Bailey's party than conjugating irregular verbs. "So can you believe what Jessica was wearing last night?" asked Bailey while the girls reviewed *le subjonctif*.

"Yes!" responded Lainey a little bit more enthusiastically than she had intended.

"Can you believe her parents let her wear a nude bandage dress with those sky-high heels from Steve Madden? They were literally six inches tall. Why does her mom let her dress like some sort of street walker from LA?" Bailey punctuated her statement with a giggle.

"Didn't Jessica's mom die of breast cancer last summer?" Allie asked, looking Bailey pointedly in the eye. Allie actually knew for a fact this was the case. Jessica's mother had worked at the same law firm as Allie's dad, so the Dennings had all attended the funeral as a family. She had almost nothing in common with Jessica Lewis, a champion equestrian who spent all of her time outside school at the Country Club with her horse, Nemo; however, Jessica had never said a mean word to Allie or any of her friends. Besides, Allie was much more offended by underage drinking than grieving girls in bandage dresses. She was selectively puritanical.

"Oh, I forgot," conceded Bailey. "Even so, the woman still had a good fifteen years to teach her daughter how to dress tastefully. I think she kind of dropped the ball in that department."

"I sort of liked the dress," interjected Lainey. "Jessica is really toned from all the riding. I loved how it fit her."

"Okay, perv. Don't go all Sapphic on us, Lainey," laughed Bailey.

Just then, a text flashed up on Lainey's iPhone. The girls roared when they saw that it was from "Your Boyfriend." You see, Teddy St. Germaine had programmed his contact information into Lainey's cell the night before when she was drunk off three-quarters of a cooler, and had clearly taken liberties with his namesake.

"Oh my God! Teddy just messaged you," shrieked Bailey in enthusiastic tones. She sounded more excited now than she had when her parents presented her with their birthday gift the night before: a brand new, bright red mini cooper. "Tell us what it says!" She insisted. Bailey had no intention of being left out of the loop.

Lainey did not want to read the text at all, let alone in front of her two best friends. What on earth could Teddy want from her? Lainey was at a loss. Yes, she had drunkenly gotten into some interesting situations the night before, but everyone knew Lainey was not exactly experienced.

Every prep school girl in the greater Boston area was well aware that Teddy was only interested in girls for sexy sorts of encounters. He was not one to take a girl out for dinner and a movie. Lainey was pretty sure that he must be feigning interest in her as a prank.

Unfortunately for Lainey, Bailey was desperate to read the message. Even though Austin was the sort of boyfriend her parents had always wanted her to be with – clean-cut, well-mannered and politically connected with a grandfather who was a senator – she had always had a crush on Teddy.

He was dangerous, roaming around town with the top down on the black BMW convertible his family gave him when he turned sixteen. His parents did not seem to care at all about his curfew, and since he looked a good five years older than he was, he took advantage of this freedom to go drinking at the trendiest bars in Boston. At such establishments, Teddy frequently picked up pretty girls from Boston University before heading back to their dorm rooms.

If Bailey had been honest with herself, she would have admitted she was jealous of Lainey for attracting Teddy's attentions, but self-reflexivity was not one of her strong points. So instead she aggressively grabbed Lainey's phone and began to read the message aloud.

Bailey recited Teddy's words in a deep, raspy imitation of his voice. "'Hey there, Lainey! I just wanted to say you looked really hot last night. I like the way your clothes leave something to the imagination, like you're a Geisha or something. How about I take you out for drinks at the Liberty Hotel some time this week?'" When Bailey was done reading, she gave her signature high-pitched squeal. No one was ever quite sure if it was a squeal of delight or one of horror.

"So, are you going to go?" asked Allie. She was wary of Teddy, as he had quite the reputation. Yet, a small part of Allie was envious of her friend. Allie was far from boy crazy and likely would never have been able to find the time to see a boyfriend if she did have one. At the same time, a tiny part of her desired confirmation that having a boyfriend was an option, just in case she ever did decide she wanted one. Of course, Allie knew boyfriends were not the be-all and end-all. It was just hard to remember that sometimes, like when all of her friends had become so boy crazy.

"Of course Lainey is going to go!" exclaimed Bailey before Lainey herself could answer.

Lainey knew she was trapped. How could she get out of this evening with Teddy now? She thought back to the night before, with Imogene. Imogene really liked Teddy. She had been desperate to attract his attention, and Lainey did not want to upset Imogene. But Lainey also knew it was difficult to argue with Bailey. She was more stubborn than a poorly trained terrier. As children, she had always managed to force Lainey and Allie to watch *Hannah Montana* at sleepovers.

"I am not sure how I feel about Teddy," said Lainey cautiously. "So I may refuse him."

"You 'may refuse him?'" responded Bailey in a mocking voice. "Who are you? Elizabeth Bennett?" In truth, that was exactly who she was emulating. Almost everything Lainey knew about relationships between men and women she had learned from Jane Austen novels.

Bailey was baffled by Lainey's reluctance. She cried, "You're going, duh! It's Teddy St. Germaine, the hottest guy under eighteen in the Greater Boston area. Plus, he has that convertible, which is so on point. Almost every other guy at Hillsview drives a boring Prius."

"Bailey, I know you're just trying to encourage Lainey to do what you believe will make her happy, but ultimately, Lainey knows herself best. It's her choice. She can date whomever she likes," interjected Allie, trying to be diplomatic. Of course, she did have ulterior motives. Allie wasn't sure if she was ready to be in a friend group where everyone had a boyfriend but her. She feared Lainey would become less interested in their friendship if she had a boyfriend. After all, that was exactly what had happened when Bailey first got together with Austin.

For her part, Lainey felt annoyed. She had always been the least talkative of the three girls, but she hated the tendency Allie and Bailey had to speak about her like she could not speak for herself.

Lainey thought back to the night before, when she and Imogene made out with each other in order to titillate Teddy. She could vividly remember the feeling of Imogene's soft lips as Teddy and his friends from Hillsview cheered them on.

"I don't want Imogene to get mad at me. She likes Teddy," murmured Lainey, quietly. She avoided eye contact with her friends as she shared these feelings. She knew how they felt about Imogene, who had been the class bully since birth. In grade two, during arts and craft, Imogene had gone so far as to cut one of the blonde ringlets out of an unsuspecting Bailey's hair with a pair of scissors. The two had been sworn enemies ever since.

"The fact that Imogene wants him makes it even better. I hate her!" declared Bailey decisively.

"I assumed your feelings towards her had thawed somewhat?" asked a confused Allie. "You invited her to your birthday party. Why would you do that if you hate her so much?"

"My mother always says that making a guest list for an important event has nothing to do with who your friends are," replied a smug Bailey.

It was true that Babe Holbeck had been teaching her children the rules of Southern etiquette since infancy. According to Babe, a true Southern Belle never showed any weakness. To deny Imogene an invitation when the entire class was supposedly invited would have been to admit that Imogene had succeeded in getting under Bailey's skin. Babe Holbeck's understanding of decorum had more to do with Sun Tzu's *The Art of War* than the writings of Emily Post.

Bailey was determined that if she herself would never know what it was like to have a long, lingering make out session with the hottest guy at Hillsview, her nemesis Imogene Butler-Thompson must also be denied the opportunity. Because of that, even though she was somewhat jealous that one of her oldest friends would probably soon go to second base with her crush, she didn't care. Bailey was keen to get Teddy embroiled in a relationship with Lainey to keep him safely out of Imogene's hot pink manicured hands.

Still holding Lainey's phone, Bailey issued the following decree: "If you won't text him back to say yes, then I will!"

"Please don't!" cried out Lainey in desperation. For just a moment, she thought she might have an honest-to-goodness panic attack.

"That is not cool!" echoed Allie.

"Trust me, it's like, for your own good. What kind of normal teenage girl doesn't want to go out with a guy like Teddy?" demanded Bailey.

Allie was about to embark upon a diatribe about how many women steer away from womanizers, and for good reason. Before she could, however, Lainey jumped in.

"You're right, Bailes!" she shrieked. "I'll go out with him!"

And just like that, the debate over whether Lainey should date Teddy was over as quickly as it began.

Octavia was prepared to admit that, despite her best efforts, she wasn't a perfect long-distance girlfriend. For the first week she'd been in Boston, Octavia spent every waking minute waiting for a text or a call from Marcus. She sent him silly photos on Snapchat throughout the day, and texted "I love you" first thing when she woke up every morning.

Lately, however, things had been busier. Octavia used to feel bereft when Marcus said he didn't have time to FaceTime with her, but now she was the one turning down Marcus' offers of video chatting. Of course, there was debating. That monopolized a good deal of her time. However, Octavia was finding that her extra-curricular work had sparked her interest in other homework as well. All of a sudden, she was researching history essays on the treaty of Versailles and worrying what would happen if the polar ice caps melted.

There just wasn't time anymore for long, lingering phone calls, or to send Marcus Snapchats of her making silly faces with a Pumpkin Spice Latte.

So two days after Bailey's birthday, when Marcus texted to say "We need to talk," Octavia couldn't exactly blame him.

Octavia hesitated for a minute before responding. Was this

the end, she wondered? Was Marcus finally through with her? Her stomach sank. How had she let this happen? How had she allowed herself to start ignoring the person she had thought was her true love for most of her life?

"You're right," she texted back, hoping she could save their relationship by saying the right things. "Would you like me to FaceTime you?"

"No, I want to speak to you in person. I want to hold you close and kiss you all night."

Octavia was almost reduced to tears by the sentiment. "I want that too, Marcus. I want that so much, but you're in Montreal and I'm in Boston." She was worried this meant the end. If she couldn't be near her boyfriend, maybe he didn't want to be with her anymore.

Thirty seconds later, Octavia's phone pinged again. The message read, "That's okay, I came to you. I'm right outside your room. Let me in!"

Octavia was in shock. Would Marcus really do something so rash? Did he know the kind of trouble Octavia would be in if she was caught with a boy in her room? Surely this was a practical joke. Surely Marcus would never do something so ... thoughtless.

Octavia opened the door to her room just to be sure Marcus was kidding, but lo and behold, he was standing right there. "Oh my God!" she cried in panic. Luckily Octavia thought to pull him inside her room before anyone saw. By a stroke of luck, her roommate was out of town for a jazz band competition in New York. She had left this morning and would be gone for almost two days.

"You can't be here!" shrieked Octavia once they were both in the safety of her room. "What if someone saw you? Having a boy in your room is verboten here. I could get in so much trouble for this!"

"What's the worst that could happen?" responded Marcus, placing his hands firmly around Octavia's waist. "I mean, don't we want you to get in lots of trouble? If you got kicked out, you could come home to me."

Octavia unfurled Marcus' hands from her body. "I don't want to get expelled. You know that would go on my record. I would never get into a good university if that happened."

Marcus chuckled. "Whoa, who are you and what have you done with my girlfriend? Who is this Type A freak who's so worried about her future?" he teased. Marcus put down his duffle bag and leaned in for a kiss, but Octavia walked away. She flopped down on her bed, feeling too overwhelmed to stand on her own two feet. She didn't want to tell Marcus to leave, but she was terrified of what would happen if he stayed. This was a bit of a conundrum.

Marcus lay down on the bed next to Octavia. He grabbed one of her tendrils and began to twirl it between his fingers. "Tavy, this is a good thing. I missed you. I wanted to be near you, to talk to you. Maybe to do things we never got a chance to do back home?" He gave her a meaningful glance. Oh no, thought Octavia, was he talking about sex?

It wasn't that Octavia had never thought about losing her virginity with Marcus. She had, a lot. But right now she was too stressed to consider it. She imagined her first time as something that would be meticulously planned out and memorable. Octavia used to believe she would have her first time at her father's country house some weekend when no one was there. She imagined lighting candles, listening to Ella Fitzgerald, and kissing vigorously by the fire. She hadn't envisioned a hasty and spontaneous experience on the single bed of her residence room at ABC.

Still, Octavia didn't want to lose Marcus. That was one thing she knew. This was the boy she had obsessed over for years. She couldn't lose him over something like this. Not when Octavia had thought he was the boy she would marry since she was a little girl.

Octavia put on a beguiling smile and took a deep breath.

She was about to start her charm offensive. Octavia cooed, "Marcus, I'm sorry I was surprised at first. I'm really happy to see you, but ah, if you're going to stay, can we just kiss and cuddle?" Octavia thought it was best to let him know right away; however, she tempered the announcement by flirtatiously stroking his chest.

"I thought you were ready, Tavy." Octavia was not sure what had given Marcus that impression. They had never discussed having sex before.

"I am. I mean, I ALMOST am," replied a very flustered Octavia. "I just ... I don't want it to be here, in my dorm room. It's not romantic, is it?" She hoped Marcus would be sympathetic to this. "We're surrounded by all my homework and my text books. How am I supposed to get in the mood for something like that here?"

Marcus opened his messenger bag. "Well, I come bearing gifts, including your favourite brand of vodka and all the fixings for martinis. That will get us nice and relaxed."

"You brought what?" Octavia grabbed the bottle and hurriedly put it in the secret compartment of her armoire. "Marcus, having alcohol on ABC property is a serious offense! How much trouble are you trying to get me into?"

"Tavy, don't freak out. I'm trying to be a good boyfriend. I came all this way to surprise you. I even brought you a freaking gift. Plus, I thought you wanted to go further." Marcus paused, his cheeks were red with rage. For the first time, Octavia actually felt afraid of him.

Marcus, however, was not done his rant: "Were you lying when you said you wanted to be my girlfriend? Because you seem to have no interest in sleeping with me whatsoever! Do you even want to be in this relationship at all?"

Octavia was desperate to calm Marcus down. She tried to reason with him. "Marcus, I always envisioned us having our first time in the woods, by the lake, or at least at a suite in the Ritz-Carlton. Just because I don't feel comfortable having my first time in my boarding school dorm room doesn't mean I'm not attracted to you."

Marcus immediately retorted, "Yeah, but if we wait to be somewhere romantic, I could be waiting for months! You aren't coming home again for a while!"

Octavia knew it was time to up her game. She gave Marcus a long, passionate kiss. The kind people have in movies; however, in this case, it was more of a diversion tactic than an act of love. After the kiss was done, Octavia whispered in his ear, "Marcus, I promise you that it will be worth waiting for."

He didn't reply, but he did wink at her. Octavia felt relieved. She had won this battle. Marcus seemed placated for now. He seemed to have stopped his Incredible Hulk impression and become her charming boyfriend once more.

For the rest of the evening, Marcus and Octavia lay spooning on her bed, intermittently making out and watching old episodes of *Arrested Development* on Octavia's laptop.

Still, despite having won this particular conflict with Marcus, she knew he was likely not done with the war. Octavia felt confused. She wondered, "How can the boy I love be so scary sometimes? Is that normal?" In response, a small voice in her head that Octavia wished she could ignore responded with an emphatic, "No!"

10.

THE BOYFRIEND'S BACK

WITH NINE DAYS to go before the Howard Cup, debate practice was ratcheting up yet another notch. The tournament was in parliamentary debate style, which involved a team of two debaters arguing in favour of the resolution, who were known as the government team, and a team of two more opposing it, known as the opposition. Over the course of the tournament, Octavia and Allie would have to debate both sides of the resolution. Each side would take turns speaking, concluding in a rebuttal from the government side. Octavia had now accepted that debate was a ton of work. She wouldn't admit as much to Allie, but she was eager to amass as much information as she could before the tournament.

The only problem was that Marcus was still in town, and he was being equally intense about his need to monopolize her. That morning, when they had FaceTimed, Octavia convinced Marcus she had to attend classes and debate practices to avoid arousing the suspicions of her teachers and coaches, but she knew he could only be expected to hide out in his hotel room playing Candy Crush for so long. Marcus was getting impatient. He had skipped a couple days of classes at McGill to spend time with her, and Octavia knew Marcus expected a worthwhile return on his investment. So far, she was managing to appease Marcus with long make out sessions when he visited her in the evenings, but she could tell he was unsatisfied when she snuck him out before going to bed each night. He was still lobbying Octavia to go all the way.

Every time Octavia snuck a look at her iPhone, a new text from Marcus popped up. At first, his texts were sweet: "Hey babe, I miss you!" Soon, however, they became more questioning: "Octavia, how long can a high school debating practice last?" and finally, Marcus' messages became somewhat threatening: "Tavy, I flew in all the way from Montreal to surprise you. I refuse to be treated this way."

Octavia tried to explain to Marcus how important it was to prepare for The Howard Cup, but he could not grasp how an extra-curricular could mean so much to her. He thought Octavia was just looking for excuses to get out of spending time with him. He'd said as much the night before over Face-Time, "Tavy, I think you're just searching for stupid reasons not to hang out with me! Is there another guy you're seeing or something?" Octavia reassured Marcus this was not the case, but she wasn't sure he believed her.

Now, two hours after school ended on a Monday, Octavia and Allie had only just finished a practice debate against Bailey and Lainey. For this round of parliamentary debate, Octavia and Allie were the opposition team to Bailey and Lainey's government team.

Since Octavia had never been to an actual debate tournament before, Jack was keen to get her up and speaking as much as possible before the big event. Jack believed in Octavia, and definitely wanted to bring out the best in her, but if he were being completely honest with himself, Jack's attempts to cultivate his new student were mostly motivated by a desire not to fail Allie.

Whatever Jack's motivation, he had little to fear. It was obvious to all that Octavia was coming along as a speaker. She was not nervous in the slightest when she delivered speeches about complicated matters of international relations. To the contrary, at recent practices, Octavia was proving to be engaging and informative. She made eye contact with her audience, modulated her voice in a dramatic manner, and had learned a lot of useful facts about the resolution on whether Turkey should be admitted into the EU. Jack knew she'd be a pro with a bit more practice.

Jack and Anna were seated in the front row of the ABC debates room taking notes on the girls' speeches. They had already finished one round of debate and were started on another one for good measure.

Rajeev Lahiri, however, was noticeably absent. He was still driving back from New York with Melissa. That weekend, they had attended the wedding of her friend Genevieve, a former fashion model who moved to New York to marry the head of a successful hedge fund.

For this practice session, Lainey acted as the first government speaker so she kicked off the debate. While her speech was full of excellent research, Lainey had a tendency, even when speaking to an audience, to talk quietly, and in a somewhat robotic tone. Though whip smart, anyone could see Lainey lacked a real passion for public speaking. The truth was debating was not an activity Lainey participated in by choice. Her parents had forced their daughter into it in middle school in a fruitless effort to bring her out of her shell. They had no idea why their beautiful and brainy daughter seemed so uncomfortable in her own skin. Still, they were determined to mould her into someone with the pathological self-confidence of Mitt Romney, but with less plastic-looking hair. Honing Lainey's public speaking skills was part of this plan. Now Lainey feared she would be stuck with the activity forever.

Though she loved Lainey more than any friend she'd ever had, listening to her Prime Minister's speech made Allie feel for the first time that Jack had been right to force her to debate with Octavia. For the first time, Allie could see Lainey's heart wasn't in debating the same way it was with things she truly loved, like working on the school yearbook or writing hard news stories for the ABC newspaper. Allie began to feel like a bad friend for not having noticed it sooner.

By contrast, Allie noticed Octavia seemed to light up when she delivered a speech. And whether she admitted it to Allie or not, it was obvious Octavia had started spending lots of her free time researching Turkish politics. Allie felt her resentment toward Octavia begin to fade away. Slowly but surely, these feelings of resentment were being replaced by a grudging respect for Octavia Irving.

Allie did not know, however, that Marcus had just flown into town. While Allie was no longer so anxious about the idea of debating with Octavia, Allie was by no means close to her. The only time the two girls had ever in theory socialized together outside of school was at Bailey's sweet sixteen the weekend before, and that hardly counted, as Allie spent most of the night in an empty Jacuzzi reading *Hard Choices*.

Allie was fairly certain she would never be FRIENDS with Octavia. After all, besides the exceptional circumstances of Bailey's birthday, neither she nor any of her friends usually frequented raucous parties featuring drugs and public foreplay. Even if Lainey was supposed to be going on a date with the most notorious teenage playboy in Boston, Allie considered her friendship circle to be the "good girls" of the tenth grade at ABC. She wasn't certain exactly what that meant anymore, but she was sure the label wouldn't apply to Octavia.

After Lainey, it was Octavia's turn to deliver her speech. Just as she was about to open her mouth, however, she caught sight of something unwelcome. It was Marcus passing by the large rectangular windows of The ABC Debates Room when he was supposed to be safely ensconced in his hotel room, where no one could catch site of him.

Not only was Marcus out and about on the ABC campus, but he was dragging his green compact Tumi suitcase with him. This was serious. Octavia's heart sank into her stomach. Was Marcus, the love of her young life, about to abandon her in some fit of fury? Octavia knew if she allowed Marcus to walk out now, there was a good chance they would break up. She was convinced Marcus had a good heart, but anyone would admit he was temperamental. Marcus loved Octavia, of this she was certain, but she also knew he expected to be the centre of her universe in return. Because she had spent her entire life fantasizing about being with him, when Marcus finally noticed her six months ago, the fact he demanded so much attention seemed like a small price to pay. After all, in her old life in Montreal, Octavia had cared about little besides Marcus, anyway.

Luckily, no one else had yet noticed Marcus' figure in the window, trailing his luggage. This was basically a miracle, as a boy on the ABC campus who was dressed in anything other than a Hillsview Prep uniform normally caused quite the commotion.

Without a word of explanation, Octavia ran out of the room to find Marcus. She didn't know how she'd explain the incident later, and she didn't care. In that moment, all that mattered to Octavia was getting to her boyfriend.

As soon as Octavia fled the room, Bailey shrieked, "Well, that was rude!"

"Bailes, don't be mean," chided Lainey under her breath. As someone who had been afflicted by stage fright her whole life, she was somewhat sympathetic to Octavia's departure. Lainey simply assumed Octavia had developed a sudden case of uncontrollable nerves.

Anna, who was always very good when other people were in crisis, excused herself right away to follow Octavia. By contrast, Jack was stunned and somewhat at a loss for what to do next. He sat in silence for a minute or two as the girls just stared at him, waiting for their coach to give them some indication as to how they should proceed.

After several minutes, it became obvious that neither Octavia nor Anna were returning any time soon.

"Okay, I guess we aren't going to finish the debate today," said Jack. He was wearing a somewhat bemused expression. "So, you guys can stay and I can look over your research notes with you," he continued. "Or, I guess you can just go home now and start enjoying your evening."

With no hesitation, Lainey and Bailey opted for the latter option, immediately heading out the door. Allie, however, was always up for more preparation. She was also hoping that Octavia would return soon with an explanation as to why she'd fled. Allie desperately wanted there to be a good justification for her disappearance. She needed to be certain her debate partner was reliable and committed to their partnership, even if the evidence before her seemed to suggest this wasn't true. Octavia was still the same girl who had not wanted to do research with her the week before. For all of her charisma as a speaker, Allie feared the girl still did not take debating seriously.

"Where are you going?" Octavia called to Marcus in a frantic tone. She was slightly out of breath. She'd had run to catch up with him. Marcus was almost at the Norton Gates, the imposing stone pillars and wrought iron fence that separated ABC's campus from the rest of Mission Hill.

Marcus stopped in his tracks and turned around. "Hi. I just came to your dorm room to say goodbye," he said with an affected coldness.

Octavia sensed now that if she wasn't careful with what she said, she could lose Marcus in an instant. "Marcus, don't leave. You're angry. Let's talk about this. I didn't mean to ignore you. You're right, it's sweet that you came to visit me!" Octavia wasn't sure she believed everything she was saying, but she was desperate to placate her boyfriend anyway.

"And whose fault is it that you have no time to spend with me?" spat Marcus angrily.

"Marcus, I love you. I love you so much! I just had no idea

you were coming this weekend. I'm sorry. I have these after school commitments and I can't break them. Just because I can't spend all my time with you, it doesn't mean I don't love you!" Octavia was on the verge of tears now.

"The old Tavy would have skipped school to hang out with me if I asked her to, and she definitely would not have prioritized some nerdy debating practice over our relationship." Marcus paused for a second, before adding, "I don't think you do love me anymore."

Marcus' words hit Octavia like a bullet to the heart. Perhaps she was busier than she had been in the past. Sure, the distance meant they were spending less time together, but how could Marcus seriously doubt her feelings for him when Octavia had never loved anyone but him?

Octavia's eyes filled with tears. Ever since she was a child, she had rarely cried. It always seemed like such a dramatic waste of time. Yet now, on the verge of losing her beloved, the tears poured out without Octavia even realizing it.

Just then, Octavia and Marcus noticed a figure coming right towards them. In a second, Octavia registered the approaching young woman in a navy blue wrap dress as Ms. Knole.

"What is going on here?" demanded Anna when she was close enough to be heard.

Octavia said nothing. She silently stared at the ground, willing Anna to go away.

"I'm trying to talk to my girlfriend," Marcus told Anna with a hostile stare. "So could you please give us a minute?"

At that moment, Anna seemed to morph into a completely different person. Her posture became more erect and she glared at Marcus through narrowed eyes. "You do not speak to me that way!" Anna said firmly. She did not raise her voice but managed to sound authoritative anyway.

"I am Octavia's guidance counsellor and I have every right to be here," continued Anna with conviction. "You, however, have no reason to be on ABC property and so I must kindly ask you to take your suitcase and leave. Please hurry before anyone sees you too. Do you have any idea how much trouble you could get Octavia into by being here?"

"What are you, some sort of goddamn Nazi," asked an irritated Marcus. He wasn't in the habit of following orders from people, even when they were in the right.

"My father is Jewish and so is your girlfriend. That is an incredibly culturally insensitive thing to say. Please leave before I have to call security."

"Whatever, I don't even want to be here anyway." Marcus turned and walked away from the ABC campus without once looking back at Octavia.

As soon as Marcus was out of sight, Anna turned to her student. At this point Octavia was sobbing uncontrollably. It was obvious Anna could not take her back to debate practice until Octavia had calmed down. One look at her and everyone would know that something was up. Anna, of course, felt reasonably sure that Marcus had been in Octavia's room at some point, judging from his suitcase. However, since she had no actual proof, Anna decided it was not necessary to notify Headmistress Carole. "Come on," said Anna to Octavia giving her a pat on the back. "It's five-thirty. The staff room will be empty by now, so let's go there and talk. I can make you an espresso."

Octavia gave her guidance counsellor a confused look. "I thought coffee for students was not allowed at this school?"

Anna smiled warmly. "I think we can make an exception this one time."

"So I think we can argue that Turkey is definitely becoming less secular. I mean, women can now wear hijabs to universities, which they were not able to do before," said Allie, making a note of this idea in her debate binder.

"You don't think it's possible to have a secular society where women can wear whatever they want to school, including religious garb?" asked Jack. He got up and moved to the seat beside Allie.

"Well, of course you can have a secular government that allows its people to have religious expression. I guess what I'm noticing is how Turkey's own approach to secularism is evolving." Allie continued to scribble down notes.

"Um, wait! What is that?" gasped Jack out of nowhere.

"What is what? Stop distracting me. I'm trying to expand my case notes."

"The way you hold your pencil! I can't believe you don't realize how weird that is!" Jack was gesticulating wildly to hammer home his point. In truth, Allie did not hold her pencil in the traditional way. Rather than pinching a pencil between two fingers gingerly, Allie grabbed it in a clenched half first.

"My penmanship is fine so my parents and teachers never really cared. Honestly, why does it matter?" Allie demanded.

"It just looks wrong!" Jack insisted vehemently. He grabbed Allie's hand, positioned her fingers around her pencil as he saw fit, and said, "Come on, I'll guide you. I'm not moving my hand until you show me you can write in the proper position."

Allie had never before held hands with a boy. Her heart quickened a little at the feeling of Jack's fingers on hers. Of course, she knew they were not holding hands as such. They were not couple on a date at the movies or something like that. Still, the whole situation felt much more intimate than a debate practice should.

Jack was leaning in close to Allie now. His head was so close to hers she thought she could almost taste his breath. Allie felt as if she were under a spell. She became acutely aware of Jack's slim but toned body beside hers, dressed in khakis and a salmon coloured slim fit Polo that revealed his muscular arms. For a split second, Allie thought it would be nice to have arms like Jack's wrapped around her. Without realizing it, Allie began to quiver.

"Why are you shaking?" asked Jack. He sounded genuinely concerned. This was not their customary sarcastic banter. Allie felt Jack place his free arm around her back. He began to stroke her softly.

"I must be shivering," said Allie. She was trying to affect a casual tone. "It's an awfully cold day for late September." This was a feeble excuse. Allie knew full well it was unseasonably warm. Suddenly, the door to the Debates Room opened to reveal Anna Knole. Octavia followed closely behind her, carrying what looked to be a latte. Jack and Allie froze in shock.

"We're back," called Ms. Knole cheerfully. She was self-conscious about having been absent from the practice. It was her job to supervise for the better part of an hour. Because of this, she failed to process how Jack appeared to be carrying on with one of their students.

"Sorry about that," said Octavia, trying to sound as if she had not been crying her eyes out only minutes before. "It's my time of the month and I needed to get some feminine hygiene products. Apologies to you Jack if that was TMI." She looked at Jack and Allie huddled together and added, "You two look cozy."

Jack pulled away from Allie immediately. "I'm glad you're back, Octavia. Let's get to work."

With that, everyone left in the room went back to preparing for the Howard Cup as if nothing had happened at all.

11.
GRANDMA LIKES TO PARTY

TRUDY DENNING (nee Cooke) did everything worth doing in some style. Descended from shipping magnates who grew their already considerable fortunes to unimagined heights in the early twentieth century, Trudy was old money. So old, in fact, that her parents were among the original members of America's original country club, the sprawling Boston institution known simply as *The Country Club*.

It was at The Country Club, the same location where she had been married to Allie's now deceased grandfather fifty-six years before, that Trudy decided to have her eightieth birthday celebration.

When it came to parties, Trudy left nothing to chance. An expert socialite who put the new generation of Trumps and Santo Domingos to absolute shame, Trudy Denning's style of celebration was what she referred to as, "more Kennedy and less Kardashian."

For Trudy, subtlety was paramount. Of course she believed everything ought to be the best, but there was no reason to be SHOWY about it. She was certain her idea of well-bred people, the people whose opinion she believed really counted, would notice the difference between Krug and Moët & Chandon without having to be told one was more expensive.

Being somewhat older than she was when she danced until dawn at Lee Radziwell's wedding decades before, Trudy now opted to celebrate becoming an octogenarian over a leisurely

102

luncheon. However, the grandeur of the occasion would not be lost.

All three of Trudy's grandchildren would be in attendance, even Allie's brother Aram, who had to be flown in from Stanford for the weekend. To make certain they were dressed to standard, Trudy also bought each grandchild a new outfit from Barney's on her last trip to New York. Of course, this policy was probably unnecessary where Allie's cousin Margot, a twenty-five-year-old MBA student at Harvard, was concerned.

Margot was the daughter of Allie's aunt, Lillian. Lillian, who owned an art gallery that never seemed to sell a single painting, was married to a managing partner at Boston Consulting Group named Garry Easterbrook. Appearances were important to Garry, and in this, Margot never let him down. Indeed, Margot had had a stylist approximately since birth. Margot could absolutely be trusted to attend her grandmother's fete wearing something that had been worn by Kate Middleton the week before.

The idea to buy each grandchild an outfit actually come about because Trudy was well aware her daughter-in-law Sybilla had an absolute disdain for clothes she referred to as "designer." Trudy herself could not have cared less WHO designed her grandchildren's clothes, as long as they appeared to be well made. Trudy was certain, however, that Sybilla would likely have sent her adolescent children to their grandmother's birthday in some discount, seventy-percent cotton, thirty-percent polyester monstrosities.

Rather than risk offending Sybilla by suggesting she could not be trusted to clothe her own children, Trudy informed the whole family it would mean a great deal if she could dress her beloved grandson and granddaughters on what she stressed *could easily be one of her last birthdays.* Of course, the last time Trudy had gone in for an EKG, the nurse asked her if she ran marathons, because her heart was so healthy. Trudy, however, saw no problem in harmless fibs.

When Trudy presented Allie – her favourite granddaughter even though she never would have admitted to having a preference – with a fancy new outfit, Allie was thrilled. Grandma Trudy had impeccable taste that was unfailingly on-trend.

Allie absolutely adored the Marc by Marc Jacobs party dress her grandmother purchased for her. It was knee-length and sleeveless with a bold, abstract turquoise and purple print Allie thought was tastefully eye-catching. Allie had been looking forward to donning her new garment for months, but now that the day of the party was finally here, there was one problem she had not anticipated. This problem took the form of Allie's overflowing bust.

When Grandma Trudy first brought home the dress in July, it had fit Allie perfectly. Now, two months later, Allie surveyed herself in the mirror and realized she seemed to have grown a solid few inches, but only in her breasts.

Allie, who was a moderate B-Cup for the previous two years, was suddenly gifted with a not inconsiderable amount of cleavage. She flushed red at her own reflection in the mirror. This was not how one was meant to dress for one's grandmother's eightieth birthday party at an elite Boston country club!

Still, Allie also knew her grandmother would be deeply offended if she showed up in another dress with more fabric in the bosom without any explanation for the change. She did consider phoning Trudy to tell her the truth, that she had somehow grown a full cup size in the last couple of months without realizing it, and that she needed to wear a looser dress to compensate. Unfortunately, this plan would have required Allie to talk about her woman parts with her grandmother, and this was something of which she did not believe herself capable. Allie had no choice. She entered The Country Club that afternoon looking like someone it had never occurred to Allie the self-proclaimed "good girl" that she could be: a curvaceous woman who resembled Marilyn Monroe much more closely than she did Jackie O.

Aram and Allie knew the party, full as it was with an endless array of elderly Kennedys, Romneys, and Radziwells, was not going to be super scintillating. While Trudy was quite active, many of her friends spent their time discussing hip replacements and which Mission Hill restaurants offered dinner service at four-thirty p.m. Thankfully, Jack Mansbridge had been invited also.

The Mansbridges were long-time friends of the Dennings. In fact, Jack's grandfather had been Allie's grandfather's best man when he married Trudy. For this reason, Grandma Trudy was thrilled when her grandson became best friends with Jack when they were five years old. Jack, however, was not invited to Trudy's party solely because of his long-time family connections to the Dennings – Trudy also thought he was absolutely adorable!

When Jack arrived, Aram and Allie were crowded around the oyster buffet, trying to avoid getting into any conversations with their grandmother's more Republican friends. Those conversations never seemed to go well for Allie, who staunchly believed corporate America should pay higher taxes.

Naturally, Aram was excited to see his best friend Jack. Back when they were at Hillsview, the two hung out pretty much all day, every day. Now that Aram was studying engineering on the West Coast, their communication was reduced to hurried WhatsApp messages they sent between classes about keg parties and cute girls.

As much as Jack had been looking forwarded to reuniting with his buddy Aram, he was, however, distracted by something unexpected as soon as he entered the room: Allie Denning looked breathtaking. Of course, Jack had always known Allie was a pleasant looking girl. In recent months, if she had not been the little sister of his best friend, Jack would even have categorized her as "totally cute." Her alert hazel eyes and endearingly furrowed brow had always seemed objectively appealing. Jack had always known Allie's skin was a creamy alabaster and he probably suspected her figure, underneath the layers of the ABC uniform, was pleasing enough. But today was different. Today, all of Allie's charms seemed to be on display.

Jack approached the siblings almost bashfully. "Hey dude! It's been forever!" The two boys embraced in what they referred to as a bro hug. "Oh and Allie, hello to you too," added Jack with what he hoped was a casual nod.

"Hi Jack. You should really try an oyster. They're incredibly fresh," offered Allie in complete innocence. Jack declined politely, as the last thing he felt he needed that moment was food famous for being an aphrodisiac.

"Okay, Jack, let's ditch the little sis and go have a bromantic time!" Aram said enthusiastically. He didn't really feel comfortable discussing all the girls he'd had encounters with at Stanford in Allie's presence.

Before the two boys could escape the party and make their way to the vacant gazebo on the Country Club's grounds, however, Grandma Trudy noticed Jack and made a beeline for the three teens.

"Jack, how lovely to see you!" declared Trudy as she approached. She was slurring her words a bit from all the champagne.

Jack, who never failed to flirt with her good-naturedly, kissed Trudy on the cheek and cried, "Happy birthday, Mrs. Denning!"

"Oh please, call me Trudy," she answered with a naughty wink. Allie had never seen her prim and proper grandmother behave so shamelessly. She dearly hoped it was due to the liquor.

Luckily, Charles Denning was well aware of his mother's low tolerance for alcohol. Sensing Trudy was getting ever closer to propositioning a teenage boy, Charles rushed over to intervene. Sybilla followed, partly out of concern for her children, and partly because she enjoyed watching her mother-in-law behave inappropriately.

"Are we having a good time, Mother?" asked Charles in a meaningful tone.

"Of course we are!" Trudy said a little bit too loudly, revealing exactly how tipsy she was to a bevy of onlookers.

"Perhaps it's time to switch to sparkling water for a little while, Mother."

"Oh, don't be silly, Charles," hissed an irritated Trudy. She turned to her grandchildren, instructing them, "When your father turns eighty, I hope you act as the narcotics police, too. I want him to get a taste of his own medicine."

While Aram was clearly revelling in this rare moment of uninhibited euphoria on the part of his grandmother, Allie was confused and uncomfortable. Allie had spent most of her life being lectured on decorum by Trudy. So how on earth could that same woman think it was appropriate to get drunk in front of half the Kennedy clan and flirt with a Harvard freshman? Allie wasn't sure how all of this made sense.

Unfortunately for Allie, Trudy's outlandish behaviour had only just begun. She took another glass of champagne from a passing waiter's tray, and began taking healthy gulps. In between mouthfuls of champagne, she turned to Jack, pinched his cheek and said brightly, "You know, if I were sixty years younger, you'd be just my type!"

"Why sixty years younger? I like women, not girls," retorted Jack with a wink. For a moment, Allie could not decide if Jack was acting creepy or being a good sport.

"Oh, you're such a nice boy!" exclaimed Trudy, continuing to pat his cheek. In the next instance, she was summoning a waiter and requesting an entire bottle of Krug be brought over.

When the waiter appeared moments later with the champagne, Sybilla decided it was time to put her foot down since her husband had proven unable to reign in his mother. "Trudy, it is now definitely time to stop." Trudy glared at her daughter-in-law. She had never much cared for her. The woman was such a downer. Any time she came to the Country Club, she felt compelled to bring up how her ancestors would never have been admitted because of their Lebanese ethnicity.

Trudy felt a sudden desire to up the ante on her daughter-in-law. If she was cut off from drinking, she would obey, but in a way that maximized the potential for angering Sybilla. Trudy reached over to grab the bottle of chilled Krug from the silver bucket of ice the waiter had delivered.

"Here you go, Jack! You and Aram go have fun, compliments of Grandma Trudy!" The boys were off with their bottle in a flash, as Charles, Sybilla and Allie gaped.

"Mother, those boys are minors. You cannot give them champagne," Charles told her adamantly.

"Why not? Sybilla is always going on about how hypocritical it is that, in America, an eighteen-year-old can die in a war but can't have a drink before doing so."

Sybilla gritted her teeth. She had indeed said that many times, back before she had an actual eighteen-year-old of her own. Sybilla did not want to admit to her mother-in-law that she had become a hypocrite regarding her views on young people's drinking; however, she also did not trust Aram with an entire bottle of champagne.

Sybilla vividly remembered how, after his high school graduation, Aram enjoyed too much beer, then twisted his ankle doing "Gangnam Style." Aram had been so drunk when Sybilla picked him up from the emergency room he did not even have the good sense to lie. Instead, he shared every lurid detail with his mother, including how many keg stands he remembered doing.

When it came down to it, Sybilla was a realist. While Aram was brilliant academically, he was not exactly sensible. Allie, on the contrary, was Charles and Sybilla's little narc. There was no reason to believe she would ever get up the gumption to misbehave.

As soon as Trudy went to powder her nose, Sybilla took her daughter discretely aside and gave her a top-secret assignment

"Listen, you know that Aram cannot hold his alcohol to save his life."

"Yes," replied Allie frankly.

"Well, your mission, should you choose to accept it, is to go find the boys and make sure they don't get into any trouble," Sybilla told her daughter conspiratorially.

Allie accepted without hesitation. The thought of being in charge of her older brother was a fantasy come alive for a control freak like her.

When Allie found Jack and Aram, they were passing around the bottle of Krug on a bench near the club's duck pond. The boys were already looking dishevelled, their ties loosened and their suit jackets disposed of on the ground.

Before she even said hello, Allie scolded her brother. "Aram, that is a brand new Zegna suit Grandma bought you! How can you just carelessly leave pieces of it on the grass like that?"

"Calm down, Allie! Come here. Join us! Have your first glass of champagne! I won't tell anyone my prissy little sister indulged herself this one time."

Allie was taken aback by Aram's words. She adored her older brother, but she was starting to consider him a mean drunk.

"Just because I respect drinking ordinances does NOT make me a priss." Allie stood with her hands sassily on her hips, which Jack noticed highlighted her hourglass figure. Allie's hair was also blowing in the late September breeze. Jack could not remember a time when he thought anyone looked lovelier. Even her frown was somehow attractive to him. It seemed, if anything, to highlight Allie's bee-stung mouth. Something stirred inside him. After weeks of denial, Jack finally admitted the truth to himself: he wanted Alexandra Elizabeth Denning.

In his drunken haze, Jack seemed to forget about any notions of propriety he may have previously pretended to possess. He stood up, walked over to Allie, and placed his arm around her slyly. Her shoulders were bare, allowing him to put his hand directly on her soft, creamy pale skin.

Allie did not know how to react to Jack's embrace. It was so public! Her brother was right there, and anyone who may have been walking past could see. Nevertheless, despite how inappropriate it was to be embraced by one's debate coach at one's grandmother's eightieth birthday party, Allie did not pull away. She wanted the feel of Jack's arm around her even more than she wanted not to be seen with his arm around her.

Aram, drunk as he was, was not pleased to see his little sister in his best friend's grasp. At first, he tried to defuse the situation by making light of it. Aram razzed his friend, shouting, "Jack, dude, are you so drunk that you forgot that Allie is not a real girl? She's just a little robot who does lots of homework!"

Without even thinking, as happens often when one has been drinking, Jack came to Allie's defence. "Don't call her a robot!" he warned Aram firmly. "Allie is an intelligent young woman. She's just ambitious. Girls can be ambitious without being freaks."

Allie hated the idea of a man defending her honour. She also thought it incredibly bizarre that her honour needed to be defended against the slights of her own brother.

"Jack, please stop it," said Allie with self-possessed authority. "I can look after myself." With that, Allie shimmied out from under Jack's reach and retreated back to the clubhouse. So what if she hadn't completed her mother's spy mission? At least she had escaped with her dignity intact.

Jack called after Allie, apologizing (though he was not exactly certain of what he'd done wrong). Despite the fact that he implored her to stay, Allie did not look back once.

Aram awoke the morning after his grandmother's birthday bash in Jack's Harvard dorm room with the worst headache of his life. After the boys had finished their Krug by the pond, a happily drunk Trudy spotted them at the dessert buffet and snuck a thirty-year-old bottle of scotch into her grandson's hands. The rest of the night was somewhat of a blur from then on. However, Aram was fairly certain he had spent a good ten minutes yelling, "I am a dragon!" in the Harvard yard around three a.m. He smiled fondly to himself about his drunken antics.

Still, a more troubling memory was also bubbling to the surface. Aram thought back to the bottle of champagne he and his best friend of thirteen years had shared by the duck pond. He had a flash of Allie standing in a dress that did not leave as much to the imagination as her big brother would have liked. He remembered her enfolded in Jack's arms, and the image offended the hungover Aram so much it prompted him to run to the communal bathroom, where he proceeded to vomit.

Jack was woken by all the commotion. When Aram returned, he was already sitting upright in bed rubbing his tired eyes.

"Oh man, I have never felt so terrible in my life! Remind me not to mix Scotch with champagne EVER again!" said Jack with a grin that was surprisingly chipper for someone so profoundly dehydrated.

"I know, right? I mean, I was so drunk, I think I was hallucinating!" responded Aram in a voice he meant to sound casual, but contained a definite tone of hostility.

"What?" asked an incredulous Jack. "What did you hallucinate?"

"Well, I know this is totally gross, so promise me you won't puke when I say this, okay?"

"Okay."

"Well, in my drunken haze, I think I hallucinated that you'd tried to feel up my little sister by the duck pond!" said Aram with a forced laugh.

Jack was not sure what to do. Was his friend confronting him? Or was he trying to sweep the events of the other afternoon under the rug?

"Oh, ah, interesting. Yesterday is all pretty much a blur for me too. I think I blacked out completely." Jack tried to will his friend into believing him.

"Yeah, man, alcohol makes you imagine weird things, doesn't it? Because I know you would never be into Allie. I mean, she's my baby sister. She's a kid. And besides, you're her debate coach, so obviously you would never make a move on her." Aram sounded firm. More like he was issuing a threat than making observations.

"No, you're absolutely right. She's your sister. I would never even consider her that way," Jack lied.

"I know. Let's go see what this Harvard cafeteria has by way of breakfast," suggested Aram.

Neither of the boys mentioned Allie again for the rest of the day. But she was never far from their minds.

12.
THE VODKA, THE WITCH
AND THE WARDROBE

COLLEEN MALONE was a twenty-something graduate of Trinity College Dublin who had always wanted to live in Boston. She had hopes of meeting handsome young Towers who went to Harvard at nightclubs in Cambridge. In her wildest dreams, Colleen even imagined being "discovered" by a local news channel where the producers found her Irish charms particularly endearing. Colleen had fantasies of making it in America!

While she was working on getting her fledgling career in journalism off the ground, Colleen had found a job as a residence don at ABC. It was, of course, the waspiest place she had ever seen. She was fairly certain it was the sort of institution that would have written "No Irish Need Apply" as an addendum to any "Help Wanted" ad a mere ninety years ago; however, the school paid well and afforded Colleen lots of free time to pitch blog posts to Vulture.com.

The school, however, was incredibly strict about contraband in students' rooms. While Colleen herself had many fond memories of sneaking a mickey of vodka into school dances as a youth, she was vigilant about her duties at ABC. ABC provided her with free accommodations in their residence and a fairly decent salary. It was the key to all her dreams while she strove to "make it as a reporter," something even she knew almost no one had been able to accomplish since the invention of the Internet.

A major part of Colleen's job was to conduct random checks of the girls' rooms for things like alcohol, pot, and cigarettes. Even though boys were not allowed in the girls' rooms, condoms were. ABC felt that if their students were somehow able to break the school's rules by sneaking boys in without being noticed, they might as well break the rules safely. Not to mention the fact that some girls in residence wanted and did have sex with one another when the dons weren't looking.

On this particular day in early October, Colleen had just begun her checks when she arrived at Octavia and Su-Jin's room. Colleen was certain Octavia was the wily sort who would definitely find creative ways to hide forbidden fruit in her room. Colleen knew that if she didn't look thoroughly enough, her rival don, a prim Smith grad named Megan, would surely find a joint or something next time, making Colleen look completely inept. If this were to happen, she'd be out of a job at ABC, and out of a way to finance her new life. Ultimately, Colleen would be out of a dream.

"Contraband, contraband, where are you?" Colleen sang to herself as she looked under the bed and beneath pillows, each time finding nothing.

It was just as she was standing in the doorway, about to leave, that Colleen finally took real notice of the oak armoire Octavia had brought with her to ABC. It was painted a luscious turquoise, an exquisite piece of furniture that was probably worth far more than Colleen made in a year. It was the kind of piece that belonged to the sort of privileged people who had the means to keep secrets. Colleen opened the armoire door, moved the rainbow of different coloured Rag and Bone jeans to one side, and searched for a secret compartment. Sure enough she found one, and in it was the bottle of vodka Marcus had brought on his visit, the label peeling off and worse for wear.

Even when she herself was a student at ABC, Anna had never been summoned to headmistress Carole's office for a one-on-

one meeting. Being a rather paranoid person, Anna became convinced she had somehow committed a fireable offense without her knowledge. Did they know she had used the staff kitchen equipment to make Octavia Irving a latte the week before? she wondered. Could giving a student caffeine really be grounds for termination? It was with sweaty palms and a racing heart that she sat across from her boss.

"Anna, I have some news that concerns you," Headmistress Carole said ominously.

Anna merely nodded, not sure what to say.

"Vodka was found in Octavia Irving's dorm room the other day, in her armoire." Headmistress Carole frowned as if to punctuate her news.

"How do you know it was hers?" asked Anna, searching for some sort of plausible deniability.

"Because I highly doubt Su-Jin Kim would have known about the secret compartment in Octavia's armoire from Grange. Even so, when questioned, Octavia confessed that it did not belong to her roommate."

"I see," said Anna, nervous at the thought that Octavia had already been questioned.

"As Octavia's guidance counsellor, I would like you to discuss with her why she has decided to make such unwise life choices. Choices such as these are unbecoming of an ABC student."

Ms. Carole added, "Of course, Octavia will have to experience some consequences in addition to a lecture. I have yet to decide what the full weight of these consequences might be. It will depend on how the young lady conducts herself in the coming weeks."

Anna gritted her teeth. She knew ABC had a proud history of being stricter than many military schools. She also knew Headmistress Carole was committed to upholding this reputation.

"Until Octavia can grasp what it means to conduct oneself as a proper ABC student," Ms. Carole continued, "I do not believe she should be allowed to represent the school at any functions in the outside world. For the next two weeks, Octavia will have detention after school each day for an hour and a half. Further, she will not be allowed to attend ABC's annual Halloween Dance, and of course it goes without saying that she will not be allowed to represent ABC at any extra-curricular events held at other schools until I am satisfied that she has learned to behave in an appropriate manner."

Headmistress Carole was not known for doing anything halfway. Anna knew what her speech meant: Octavia was now barred from attending the Howard Cup!

Anna was deeply upset at the prospect that Octavia, simply because she had gotten up to something stupid with her friends (or possibly that shady boyfriend Marcus?), should be forbidden from attending a tournament for which she had spent weeks preparing. With only two days before the Howard Cup, it also meant there was no time to find and train a new partner for Allie, so both girls would be punished. Anna shivered at the thought of how Allie might take the news that she was out of a debating partner.

Hoping Headmistress Carole did not notice her shaking knees, Anna gathered her courage to speak. "I understand that fifteen-year-olds should not believe it is okay to have vodka on school premises, however, I do think it's worth considering that Octavia is still adjusting to life here in Boston. I know she's trying her hardest."

"I believe this punishment will help Octavia adjust," replied Ms. Carole evenly. She was not a sadistic woman. She simply had a healthy respect for the rules, and a firm conviction that nothing good had ever come from an ABC student breaking them.

"I know, and I think the detentions are a good idea. She should have time to reflect upon what she's done. I even think that it makes sense to forbid her from going to the next high school dance, but Octavia is not a bad kid. She just made a mistake. I don't know if you know, but she has been working very diligently as a member of the ABC debate team. Their first tournament is this weekend. She deserves to go."

"She broke the rules, Anna. I know you are new to teaching, but discipline will get easier as you go along," Ms. Carole said reassuringly. Anna, however, did not feel at all reassured.

"I just feel the punishment should fit the crime. And what about her debate partner, Allie Denning? What will we tell Allie?" asked Anna desperately.

"We won't have to tell her anything. As part of her punishment, I will make Octavia inform Allie of the news herself. It's all part of learning to take responsibility for her actions." Headmistress Carole paused to readjust her floral Hermès scarf. "I am sorry for Allie, of course, but I wonder why she was paired with someone so inexperienced in the first place? I hardly think even someone as accomplished as Allie could have carried such a lopsided team to victory."

Anna accepted defeat silently. There was nothing more she could do.

Octavia Irving rarely lost her cool back when she lived in Montreal. The old Octavia was invested in very little. She never studied for tests and did her homework but rarely. She didn't even care that much about her friends. Most of Octavia's close friends in Montreal had been other underachieving young women from privileged backgrounds who shared Octavia's fondness for parties and alcohol, but were not exactly Octavia's intellectual equals. Her old social group rarely talked about anything other than manicures and Drake's attractiveness.

Now that she was at ABC, everything was so much more complicated. Her once effortless relationship with Marcus seemed over, and suddenly possessing the necessary ingredients for a martini had become a serious offence. Here she was, waiting for Allie Denning to make her way to the ABC Debates Room after school in order to inform her that she, Octavia, would not be able to attend the Howard Cup. She braced herself for a lot of sanctimonious shouting on Allie's part.

When Allie entered the Debates Room, she was in good spirits. She was even whistling. Little did Octavia know that Allie always transformed into a euphorically cheerful person when a debating tournament was on the horizon. Octavia felt a pang of guilt at the thought that she would ruin Allie's day, but she tried to ignore it. Why shouldn't Allie learn to live with disappointment? thought Octavia. It was not as if she hadn't dealt with her own fair share of disappointment this past year.

Allie, suspecting nothing, was the first to speak. "Hey, Octavia!" she greeted her partner. "Jack's going to focus on giving us pointers for rebuttal speeches today. I think that will be really useful, don't you?"

"I'm not staying for practice," Octavia blurted out quickly. She was suddenly desperate to get the conversation over and done with.

"What? You have to stay! The Howard Cup is only two days away," shrieked Allie.

"I can't go to that either."

"That is not funny, Octavia. Of course you're going. Stop with these weird pranks!"

"No, they're not pranks. One of the dons found some vodka in my room. As a consequence, I can't represent ABC at the Howard Cup. I also have detention every day after school for the next month. I have to go there right now, actually. I'm only here because it was part of my punishment to tell you the news in person." Octavia was staring down at her feet. She couldn't look Allie in her wounded face.

"Why did you have alcohol in your room? You know that's not allowed. Why did you ruin this for us, Octavia? We worked so hard." Allie was the very picture of betrayal.

"My boyfriend brought the vodka when he came from Montreal to visit last weekend," Octavia continued. She was trying to seem calm and casual, as if missing the Howard Cup meant no more to her than misplacing a barrette.

Allie stared at Octavia through frustrated eyes. "So you snuck a boy *and* booze into your room?"

"You know I'm not like you, Allie. The people I hang out with like to have fun sometimes." As soon as she'd said the words, Octavia regretted them. It was below the belt. The fact that Allie didn't drink was no one's business but her own.

"You're right, you're not like me. I would never do this to someone who was counting on me. You think you're so cool because you're irresponsible and rebellious and you know how to roll a joint. Well, there's nothing cool about letting other people down, Octavia," reproached Allie.

Octavia stood silently in front of the girl who was supposed to be her partner. Until that day, it had never occurred to Octavia that her habit of breaking all the rules could affect other people. Sure, her mistakes had led to vandalized homes and ruined flower beds from raucous parties, but Octavia had never before realized that her decisions could really hurt people at their core. It was an unpleasant realization. Hurting Allie felt like a bee sting, a localized but sharp pain that was impossible to ignore.

After a long pause, Octavia managed to muster some words. "I'm sorry," she murmured.

"Don't you have a detention to be at?" Allie's icy retort let Octavia know it was definitely time to go. She slunk off to detention, cursing Anne Bradstreet College for ruining her life.

13.
SOME RULES ARE MADE TO BE BROKEN

IT WAS THE DAY before the Howard Cup, a crisp fall afternoon in early October. Allie was seated in the ABC Debates
Room, watching her friends practice for the tournament
she was no longer attending. It had been too late for Allie to
find another debate partner. However, in a cruel twist of fate,
as the ABC Debate Team captain, she was still required to attend the competition on the day to show support for the rest
of the school's debaters. All the work she had done, all the
effort she had put in, all the faith she had placed in Octavia,
was for nothing. Every time she thought about this, Allie felt
on the verge of tears.

Allie considered herself an expert on being a good girl. She
believed this meant working hard, following your teachers'
instructions, and always doing your best. Without fail, Allie
had done these things her whole life, and yet now she was
learning that in the real world, deserving something was no
guarantee of getting it.

Allie watched quietly as her friends practiced their speeches
with Jack. At first, Allie was a model of self-control. She smiled
when her friends said something intelligent and did not even
blink when they stumbled over their words. Unfortunately,
this Zen state did not last long.

By the end of Bailey's lackluster Prime Minister's rebuttal,
which was full of "likes," "ums," and the mispronounced
names of various world leaders, Allie wanted to punch herself.

Bailey had probably spent seventy-five percent less time learning about Turkey and the EU than Allie had, but she would get to represent ABC and Allie wouldn't! What made Allie even more depressed was thinking that the debaters from other schools might think Bailey and Lainey were the best team ABC had to offer. Allie worried this would cause incalculable damage to the school's honour.

Things got even more frustrating when, as soon as she was done her speech, Bailey began packing and prepared to leave.

"Don't you want to stay for some comments, Bailey?" asked Jack incredulously.

"Oh, sorry, Lainey and I have to go. We carpool and my mom has to pick me up early so we can make our weekly mother-daughter manicure appointment." Bailey seemed confident this was a good reason to skip out on debate practice early, even if they did have a tournament the very next day. Jack was about to argue with Bailey, insisting she stay, but Rajeev and Anna knew it was fruitless to cross Bailey's mother. They intervened before Jack could gather his thoughts for the lecture on the importance of practice he was preparing to give. They excused Lainey and Bailey, saying it made sense to end practice early so everyone would have enough energy to be in fighting form in the morning. Truthfully, both teachers knew it was futile to try too hard anyway. The only team they'd had high hopes for to begin with had been Allie and Octavia. Lainey and Bailey didn't want it as much, and they certainly wouldn't fight as hard to win.

After everyone else had rushed out in a hurry, excited to start their Friday nights, Allie and Jack lingered behind. Allie did so because her mother was in a meeting with a student and would not be able to pick her up for another hour, and Jack because he thought Allie looked too sad to leave alone. "Are you okay?" asked Jack when everyone else was out of earshot.

"I wasted weeks of my life preparing for something I'm not going to get to do. Of course I'm not okay!" snapped Allie.

She immediately regretted it. Jack hadn't done anything wrong. He was merely trying to be sympathetic.

"I'm sorry. You're right. That was a stupid question," he muttered.

"No, no, *I'm* sorry," insisted Allie. "That was a very unbecoming outburst." Allie paused for a second, trying to hold back her tears. "It's just not fair. I try so hard. I follow all the rules. Girls like me aren't supposed to get screwed over by the system. I mean, I practically *am* the system. What is the point of doing everything right all the time if it doesn't matter in the end?"

Jack was desperate for the right words, but everything he thought to say seemed feeble. For someone who had won awards on the basis of his eloquence, he found it ironic that when it really mattered, he was rendered speechless. After an awkwardly long silence, Jack finally spoke. "Allie, I know you did nothing to deserve this outcome. It sucks. For what it's worth, I wish this hadn't happened to you. I wish I could make it better."

"It's not your fault, Jack. You didn't hide vodka in your room, and you weren't the gung-ho don who found Octavia's secret hiding place in her outrageously expensive armoire."

"I know, but I still feel responsible. I wanted you two to debate together. It was my idea to begin with."

She could see from Jack's pained expression how guilty he felt. Allie was suddenly overcome with feelings. She could not bear the thought of having made Jack unhappy. She desperately wanted to convince him that he ought not feel guilty, that she held no grudges against him and that she knew he could not have foreseen the extent to which things would go wrong. For all his swagger, Jack now appeared exposed. He was emotionally naked in front of Allie Denning.

Allie took a couple of steps towards him, until their bodies were as close as they could possibly be without touching. Without thinking, Allie raised her hand and stroked his cheek.

Jack's smile was so warm Allie swore she could feel the heat it radiated. She studied the face before her carefully. Jack Mansbridge's curly dark hair fell over his forehead just so, and his full lips were parted slightly, as if he wanted to say something but couldn't. Allie was suddenly overcome with the desire to become familiar with his whole being.

Allie had suppressed her attraction to Jack for years. First she had denied it, because he was her brother's best friend and she knew it was inappropriate to cultivate that sort of attachment. The fact that Jack was her new debating coach just made the impossibility of them being together even more impossible. It was against the rules to like Jack – and not just the rules of ABC, the school, which paid him to teach her. It was against lots of other rules too, some of which she had set down for herself.

Allie knew Grandma Trudy would never approve because it went against the rules of propriety to like one's teacher, and she knew Charles and Sybilla would consider a relationship between their daughter and her debate coach to be a case of Jack abusing his authority. Still, if this school year had taught Allie anything, it was that behaving appropriately was no guarantee of getting what you wanted. Here she was, standing in front of Jack Mansbridge with no debate partner and a burning desire inside her body.

Allie commanded herself to stop thinking. For once, she wanted to do what she felt like doing, not what others told her she should do. She took one step closer, erasing the distance between her and Jack completely. Then, standing on her tiptoes, she reached up and kissed Jack, the only boy she had ever liked but never allowed herself to want.

Without thinking, Jack kissed Allie back. Her soft lips on his were exciting and soothing at the same time. Here was a beautiful girl who understood him perhaps better than anyone else on the planet, and she wanted him as much as he wanted her. Jack took in the smell of Allie's vanilla body wash, the feel of her soft chest against his. Each could feel the other's heart beating, and both were struck by how well their two bodies fit together.

Suddenly, their kiss was interrupted by the high-pitched ring of Allie's iPhone. Knowing it was probably Sybilla calling to inform Allie she had arrived to pick her up, Allie pulled away from Jack to answer her phone in one fluid motion.

"Hi, Mom," said Allie hurriedly. "You're here already? Oh, you're early.... No, no, no. I'm not complaining. I'm very grateful you came to pick me up. Yes, I know when you were a child you took the bus home from school each day. Yes, I know it is a forty-minute trip each way. I'll be right out."

Allie ended the call and gave Jack an apologetic look. "I'm sorry, you know how my mom is. I have to leave. Though I really don't want to," Allie flirtatiously tapped Jack's chest with her fingers. "I'll call you later! Maybe you could come over? My parents are going to the opera tonight." Allie raised her perfectly arched eyebrows provocatively.

Allie's tone was inviting, and Jack desperately wanted to say yes, but Sybilla's phone call had snapped him back to reality. This was Allie Denning, a family friend he'd known since she was born, and the baby sister of his best friend. He thought back to Aram's veiled warning to stay away from Allie the weekend before. Jack knew he and Allie could never be together.

Jack took a deep breath. He affected a serious tone. "That can never happen again, Allie."

"Ha ha, very funny."

"No, I mean it. That was really inappropriate."

Allie smirked in confusion. "But you liked it!" she said reproachfully. Allie had never been kissed before, but she was certain she knew enough to know when someone was kissing her back, and Jack Mansbridge had most definitely kissed her back.

"Allie, you're upset about not being able to go to the tournament, I get that. You're not acting like yourself. You're doing things that don't make sense. Just go home and relax tonight. You'll feel more normal in the morning."

"Jack … I don't understand," Allie protested.

"That's exactly it. You're confused. This meant nothing. Let's forget it ever happened, okay? I promise I won't tell anyone if you don't."

Allie felt as if she were having a bad dream. Everything Jack was saying made no sense. Was she so desperate to be liked by a boy that she'd imagined his interest? Had Jack's increased attentions toward her simply been a figment of her delusional imagination? She could have sworn he wanted her. Allie was a smart girl who could name all the European heads of state and every major river in Africa. How could she be so idiotic where romance was concerned? she wondered.

Quickly and wordlessly, she pulled on her backpack and walked out of the room, her cheeks burning with humiliation. How would she ever face Jack again? As Allie Denning left the halls of ABC that day, she wanted nothing more than to disappear completely.

Teddy arrived to pick Lainey up for their third date at seven p.m. the night before the Howard Cup. Normally, her parents would not have allowed Lainey to go out the night before a major extra-curricular event, but Hans and Cici decided to make an exception. Truth be told, they were delighted to see Lainey come out of her shell. They had never seen her show any interest in boys before Teddy.

When her mother and father opened the door of their Mission Hill home to meet their daughter's suitor, Lainey was upstairs pretending to be preening. The truth was that Lainey did not want to go at all. She was desperately seeking ways to procrastinate on leaving with Teddy.

On their first two outings, Lainey had used her craftiness to avoid kissing Teddy with success. It seemed he was fascinated by the Chinese aspects of her heritage. On their second date,

Teddy even went so far as to surprise Lainey by taking her to a traditional Chinese tea ceremony.

When Teddy had called Lainey the afternoon before the tea ceremony date, he declined to tell her exactly what they would be doing, preferring to keep his plans a surprise. Teddy simply told Lainey to "dress as you would for a special occasion in Hong Kong." Being a naturally obliging person, Lainey dressed up in a Balenciaga gown borrowed from her mother.

While Lainey did not particularly like the idea of being fetishized for her Asian heritage, she decided to use Teddy's tendency to do so to her advantage. Lainey invented what she referred to as "Ancient Chinese Dating Rituals," a set of fake Chinese courtship rules Teddy lapped up despite the fact that they were entirely made up.

"We cannot kiss until our thirty-seventh date," fibbed Lainey when Teddy tried to slide his arm around her waist toward the end of their first outing. "It is also forbidden to hug until the twenty-second date. Oh, and we should probably avoid holding hands for at least a few more weeks if we do not want to anger the Gods, as that would endanger the health of this year's rice crops."

"What do the Chinese Gods say about second base?" asked Teddy with a wink.

Lainey looked down at her breasts, then over to Teddy's hands. She did not want the two to mix. "Second base doesn't exist in China," she told him firmly.

Teddy sighed. "I'll miss it, but I am very much enjoying this culturally authentic experience."

Lainey was delighted by how easy it was to manipulate Teddy's casual racism to her advantage. Still, despite the fact she had successfully neutralized the threat of physical intimacy with him for the foreseeable future, Lainey felt stressed every time she went out with Teddy. This wasn't the way it was supposed to be, she knew. Teddy St. Germaine was the hottest guy at Hillsview, and he was a year older than Lainey, to boot. Dating him was a coup. And yet, on their third date, she was hiding out in her room, pretending to be touching up her makeup just to stall a little longer.

Finally, after Teddy had been waiting for a full twenty minutes, Lainey felt it was time to free him. There was only so long a seventeen-year-old boy could feign interest in Hans Eriksson's stock portfolio. As she walked down the winding staircase, Lainey could hear Teddy gamely attempting small talk with her mother. Even though she knew eavesdropping was uncouth, she stopped for a minute to listen.

"It's so sweet of you to say that!" Lainey heard her mother coo. Lainey wondered whether Teddy was chatting Cici up. She was in her forties, but she looked a lot younger. Plus, it was common knowledge Teddy had never been one to shy away from older women. A very small part of Lainey almost wished her mom would walk over to Teddy and start making out with him. Sure, it would probably have marked the end of her parents' twenty-year marriage, but Lainey was so desperate to avoid Teddy's advances that she thought it would be a reasonable price to pay.

Lainey's fantasy about her mother running off with Teddy was interrupted as Teddy spoke again. In his signature silky voice, he said, "I'm not being sweet at all, Mrs. Eriksson-Chan. It is a fact that your daughter is an amazing person. She is elegant, beautiful, and so fiercely intelligent. I feel incredibly lucky to be spending time with her."

As he praised her, Teddy sounded so genuine it made Lainey want to cry. Here was a person, however flawed he might be, who thought such nice things about her. Suddenly, Lainey felt ungrateful. She had been holed up in her room avoiding the most handsome boy she knew. He was a boy who also happened to like her enough to *wait* for her, chatting pleasantly with her parents like a pro.

When Teddy and Lainey finally left the Eriksson-Chan residence and climbed into Teddy's convertible, Lainey looked across at Teddy and felt a fondness for him she had previously not thought possible. She felt bad lying to him. Teddy, for all his foibles, was a person with a good heart. And he really liked her. She resolved to be appreciative, even though, despite her best efforts, she couldn't find him ... attractive.

Lainey took a deep breath. "You know those Ancient Chinese Dating Rituals we talked about last time I saw you?"

"Of course! And as per the rules, I will endeavour to stand at least six inches away from you at all times until our fifteenth date."

"You remembered?" Lainey was surprised how closely Teddy listened to her. "Well, it's so nice of you to be understanding, but I was thinking that maybe we could just forget about those now?"

A bewildered look came across Teddy's face. "You mean I don't have to wait thirty-four more dates to kiss you?" he asked , smiling from ear to ear.

"No, I suppose not." Lainey felt a knot form in her stomach as Teddy looked at her hungrily. Lainey told herself she had to get through this. If she let him kiss her, maybe then she'd see what all those other girls in her grade found so irresistible about Teddy. Maybe then she would finally feel normal.

"Well, I am all for being culturally sensitive, but if you want to forget the rules, I think I could be amenable." Teddy leaned forward. He was definitely going to kiss her. Lainey's heart raced uneasily. She had only kissed one other person, and that was Imogene. The kiss the two girls shared at Bailey's sweet sixteen party had been faster, wilder. It hadn't begun with this sort of incremental, interminable lean in towards her face. For some reason, Teddy seemed determined to take his time. Why couldn't he just get it over with? Lainey lamented.

Finally, Lainey couldn't take it any longer. She catapulted her face onto him, kissing him on the lips quickly. When Lainey pulled away, Teddy was dumbfounded.

The kiss only lasted a few seconds. It contained some perfunctory tongue, which Lainey hoped would make things a smidgen more interesting. Unfortunately, the whole experience underwhelmed her. Teddy, however, seemed delighted.

Lainey was the one who finally broke the silence. "Come on, let's go. We'll be late for the movie."

Teddy obliged, still smiling from ear to ear. He started his car, feeling confident he could finally rest assured that Lainey liked him back. Lainey was smiling too, but her grin was less genuine than her date's.

14.

TOUGH LOVE IS REAL LOVE TOO

A LLIE HAD PLEADED with her mother to let her skip the Howard Cup. She knew it would be easy to tell everyone a white lie. For example, Sybilla could phone the school to say Allie had eaten a bad clam the night before and given herself food poisoning. Of course, Allie knew that as the ABC Debate Team captain, it was her duty to attend even when she was not competing, to provide moral support. She knew her position as a leader meant she should rise above her feelings of self-pity to cheer on her friends and teammates. She also knew that her mother would ignore her pleading, and would never tell a white lie to save her daughter from social discomfort or embarrassment.

Today, however, Allie did not have the energy to care about the proper thing to do. Following the rules had left her with no debate partner and a whole binder full of useless research notes on Turkey and the EU. Worse, breaking the rules had resulted in her humiliation in front of Jack. Allie had concluded that she was simply the least lucky fifteen-year-old girl in the history of Boston.

Allie would have gladly skipped the tournament to ruminate over her sad fate while listening to Adele, but Sybilla put her foot down. There were parents who indulged their children when they wanted to fake sicknesses to get out of painful situations, and there were parents who did not. Allie's mother fit firmly into the latter category.

As she drove Allie to Hillsview, Sybilla scolded her pouting daughter. She chided, "Allie, it is only a debate tournament. Wipe that sour look off your face. Sometimes life is unfair. You'll have to get used to that. When I was your age, I had to work fifteen hours a week at a pizza parlour to help my family put my older brother through university. That wasn't exactly *fair*, but I got through it."

Allie hated that her mother treated misfortune like a competitive sport. Yes, Allie thought, my mom had a harder adolescence than me. Does that mean I am never entitled to feel sad about anything? Since she already felt miserable, Allie decided to risk starting a fight.

"You know, Mom, you really shouldn't complain about your childhood," Allie admonished her mother with a put on sternness. "It makes you sound so spoiled. So what, you had an after-school job! At least you got to GO to school. There are girls in Afghanistan who get killed just for trying to access basic human rights like education."

"Excuse me?" spat Sybilla. "How dare you talk to your own mother that way! You know NOTHING of how I grew up. Just because there are less fortunate people than me, that does not diminish the fact I was faced with many difficult challenges." Sybilla was irate.

"Exactly," replied Allie. "I know you grew up with lots of obstacles. I know you immigrated to this country not knowing a world of English at the age of five. I know you had to wear clothes your mother made for you. I know that your aunt cut your hair herself and that you and your siblings had to get jobs as soon as you were able." Allie was red in the face. She knew she was kicking the hornet's nest with every word she spoke, and yet she could not stop herself.

Allie grew louder as she said, "I admire how you managed to overcome all those obstacles to be the person you are, but you're still my mom. Even though my life is not as difficult as yours was, you're still supposed to care when bad things happen to me." Allie had said everything she had ever wanted to say. This rant had been at the tip of her tongue for years, but Allie had never uttered it for fear her mother would punish her for "talking back." Today, she didn't care about punishment. Allie had already lost her passion, her dignity, and the opportunity to do the one thing she had worked so hard for. It couldn't get worse. She felt untouchable.

Sybilla was quiet for several minutes, a wounded yet pensive expression on her face. Allie began to wonder if her mother would ever speak to her again. Sybilla was not one for prolonged silences, and she had never been one to run from a conflict. Plus, she always needed to have the last word.

"You think I don't care about you?" Sybilla finally demanded to know, turning to face her daughter. "If you really believe that, you are more ungrateful than I thought possible."

Allie braced herself for her mother's tirade.

"It would have been easier to leave you at home today sulking than to make you go to this tournament, Allie. I would have been able to sleep in too, which is something I never do because of your bloody extra-curriculars, which leave me running around town at all hours!" Sybilla looked meaningfully into her daughter's eyes. After a brief moment, she spoke again. "I am trying to teach you how to be a strong woman, how not to wallow in self-pity. You think I never complained to my mom about how awful my life was growing up? I did it almost every day. And you know what Grandma used to say to me? She always said, 'You think you have it so tough? When I was growing up in Lebanon my younger sister died of the flu because we couldn't afford a doctor!'" Sybilla now had tears in her eyes, which was a rarity for her. Allie had never seen her mother cry before.

Allie felt overcome by shame. She hadn't known she'd even had a great-aunt on her maternal grandmother's side, let alone that she had died of something the Boston Children's Hospital could easily treat today.

Sybilla wiped the tears from her eyes, then took a deep breath before speaking again. Her tone was gentler now. "If you ever have children, Allie, you'll learn that you have all these hopes and dreams for them. When you hold your little girl in your arms, you'll look at that sweet face, and you'll be terrified of what the world has in store for her. You'll want so desperately to protect her from everything that could hurt her, but the only way to do that is to help her grow up to be really strong." When she finished her speech, Sybilla sighed deeply before lapsing into silence. Neither mother nor daughter spoke again for the rest of the drive.

The morning of the Howard Cup, Octavia woke up at five a.m. She was so overwhelmed by guilt she hadn't been able to sleep. Octavia tried to occupy herself by rereading one of her favourite books from childhood, Mildred D. Taylor's *Roll of Thunder, Hear My Cry*. But for some reason she couldn't focus on the words on the page. She was too distracted by how much she regretted not just what she'd done to Allie, but to herself. Octavia had desperately wanted to attend the Howard Cup, even if she sometimes pretended with people like Imogene or Marcus that it wasn't that important to her.

For the first time, she wondered if it would have been better to send Marcus away when he arrived unannounced, instead of trying to make it work. *Is he really that great if he decided to ambush me out of nowhere?* The answer, Octavia concluded as she thought about the weeks of detention and silent treatment from Allie ahead of her, was decidedly "no."

At around seven-thirty a.m. Octavia's ruminations were interrupted when she heard a knock at her door. It roused Su-Jin, who looked understandably annoyed to be roused so early on a Saturday. Since she was wide awake, Octavia was the one who got up to answer it. When she did so, she was shocked to see none other than Ms. Knole.

"Good morning!" she said in a voice that was equal parts

cheerful and nervous. Her chic navy blue and white-stripped sweater was on backwards. "How fast do you think you can put on that uniform of yours?"

"Um, what are you doing here?" Octavia was stunned.

"I'm here to drive you to the Howard Cup, so we have to get going quickly or we'll miss the first round. We wouldn't want that, would we?"

Octavia felt a surge of relief. "Did Headmistress Carole change her mind about my punishment?"

"No, unfortunately she did not," Anna replied.

"Oh." Octavia was confused. "So aren't you breaking the rules by taking me?"

"Yep. So you and Allie have to win today in order to prove I made the right choice, or ... I think I'm probably going to be out of a job."

Octavia was taken aback. "You believe in me so much you'd bet your job on my performance?"

The nervousness from a minute earlier melted away. Suddenly, Anna was entirely sure of herself. Without hesitation, she looked her student squarely in the eyes, and responded, "Yes, I do."

Octavia and Anna arrived at Hillsview with only a few minutes to spare. The pair sprinted into the Great Hall, where all the action was about to begin. By the time they arrived, both student and guidance counsellor were out of breath.

The Great Hall was a sea of multicoloured kilts and blazers as young men and women who hailed from independent schools across New England milled about, waiting to debate. After scanning the length of the room, Anna and Octavia eventually spotted the ABC contingent towards the back of the throng of uniformed teens and their teachers. Anna instructed Octavia to go find Allie while she herself went to the breakfast buffet that had been set up for parents and judges. Anna was desperate to get herself a well-deserved cup of coffee. She knew that if

Headmistress Carole got wind of her actions, there would be hell to pay at any moment. In light of this, Anna figured she might as well keep herself fully caffeinated and alert in case she was about to be confronted by her enraged boss.

No one noticed Octavia approaching at first. Lainey, Bailey, Jack and Mr. Lahiri were in a heated discussion. Jack and Rajeev were obviously giving the girls last-minute advice. Allie, however, had nothing better to do than people watch as a bevy of sleepy teens reviewed their notes one last time.

When Allie noticed Octavia approaching, she thought she was seeing things. Allie had made her peace with the fact today was meant to be a lesson in how to handle disappointment. And yet, here was the perfect likeness of Octavia Irving approaching her. Surely Allie had to be imagining it. Wouldn't Octavia, who was usually glued to her iPhone, at least have texted before crashing a debate tournament she had been forbidden from attending?

"Either someone switched the lime Gatorade I just drank with absinthe and I'm hallucinating like a *Belle Époque* French painter, or you've decided to become the world's nerdiest gatecrasher!" Allie exclaimed when Octavia greeted her. Allie desperately wanted to be optimistic, to believe that Headmistress Carole had reversed her decision and allowed Octavia to debate after all. Still, she was careful not to get her hopes up. It occurred to Allie that perhaps part of Octavia's punishment was simply to witness the event from which she had been excluded?

"I'm not a gatecrasher, I'm here as a debater. I would have texted but we were really rushed and I forgot my phone in my room," said Octavia with a big and bright smile. She was sincerely happy to be there. It felt good to be able to keep her promise to Allie. It also felt good to give herself the opportunity to find out what she was capable of.

"Headmistress Carole reversed her decision?" Allie clapped with joy.

Octavia took a step closer to Allie and spoke quietly, not wanting anyone else to hear. "No, Ms. Knole just came to get me anyway. I didn't want to get her in trouble but she was pretty determined." Allie looked visibly shocked. It was one thing for teenagers to flout the rules, but adults were supposed to know better than to break protocol. Allie was decidedly baffled. She knew how serious it was for a member of the ABC faculty to defy the headmistress so flagrantly.

Still puzzled after a good thirty seconds of pondering, Allie asked Octavia, "Why would Ms. Knole risk everything just so we could debate today?"

Octavia paused for a moment, thinking before answering earnestly, "She believes in us."

15.

STEPPING UP TO THE PODIUM

O CTAVIA AND ANNA had been in such a rush to get to the tournament that, like her iPhone, Octavia had forgotten her debate notes. Out of necessity, it was therefore decided she would share Allie's.

"Okay, thank God I brought my debate binder so I could help Lainey and Bailey." Allie was grateful things were working out. She was getting excited for their first round of competition. Allie and Octavia would be opposition, arguing Turkey should not be admitted into the EU. They were debating against a government team from Dearfield.

Octavia decided to give Allie's notes a once-over before the first debate of the day. She was fairly certain she remembered all their facts and arguments reasonably well, but was determined to do her best and wanted to leave nothing to chance.

Midway through reading an argument about Turkey's human rights record, Octavia noticed in the margins a joke Allie had devised while trying to amuse herself during one of Bailey's practice speeches: "If Turkey were a nursery rhyme character, it would be little Miss Muffet; they are convinced the Kurds are in their way." Octavia laughed out loud. She had to give Allie credit: the girl was funny! Why did this playful side of her never come out when she actually debated?

"Hey, Allie." Octavia nudged her debate partner, who was engaging in yogic breathing exercises in an attempt to reach a Zen state before their first round.

Allie opened her eyes. "Yes."

"Why don't you use that joke about 'Turkey being like Little Miss Muffet' in your speech today?"

"That? That's just silly. I didn't think anyone would ever see that. I was just doodling." Allie flushed with embarrassment.

"Um, Allie. People SHOULD see this! It's funny enough to be on John Oliver!"

"No! I'm not using it in my speech. What if people don't like it? It's best to stick with the facts and sound logical reasoning. Injecting humour is always a risk. What if the audience doesn't laugh?"

"They will. This joke is a pretty brilliant play on words. It'll make us stand out," insisted Octavia, her eyes wide with enthusiasm.

"You're new so you don't get it, Octavia. That's not your fault. But trust me, I'm pretty experienced and I've done well in the past with serious speeches. Let's just stick with what works, okay?"

"Fine, but I still think the judges would like it." Octavia was a bit disappointed but did not push the issue further. She returned to reviewing Allie's very detailed notes.

Allie and Octavia's first round went extremely well. They debated two boys from Dearfield. The poor boys were in grade nine and debating for the very first time. They were so nervous they only used half their allotted speaking time. Octavia, by contrast, was a natural in her first-ever competitive round. In her speech, she brilliantly outlined the economic implications of allowing another large emerging economy into the EU before the European economy fully recovered from the financial meltdown of 2008.

Octavia's conclusion was particularly memorable. Taking turns looking each of the three judges in the eye as she stood up straight before them, waving her pointer finger for emphasis, Octavia confidently declared, "In sum, I have spoken to you about the potentially deleterious economic effects on the European Union of allowing Turkey into this organization at the present. Turkey is a beautiful country with considerable potential, but its standard of living is far below the European average. Its banking system is also not sufficiently transparent. Given the economic collapse in the PIG countries – Portugal, Italy and Greece – the EU does not have the money at present to invest in this sort of expansion. Given that so much of the EU is centred around the idea of economic partnership, bringing Turkey into its fold would be an unwise economic risk at this juncture. Thank you."

Allie was thoroughly impressed. She had never had a partner who was perhaps as good as she was. While Octavia was not as experienced and not yet quite as skilled at constructing a logical argument as Allie's past partners, her charisma and confidence made up for this in bounds. Even the driest fact about monetary policy seemed compelling in Octavia's hands.

Allie felt slightly threatened wondering if it was possible, with a little experience, that Octavia one day might surpass her in debating ability; however, Allie mostly felt relieved. Here was a partner who seemed to enjoy debate as much as she did. Maybe Octavia was not the type of girl Allie had ever been friends with or with whom she could ever see herself socializing, but Allie realized Octavia was undeniably someone she could trust. They were teammates.

The girls' second round of debate was against Poppy Foster and Noah Schwartz, a pair of well-known twelfth-grade debaters from the Hotchkiss School. This time the round was much more intense. Octavia and Allie were on Government, and while they had a great deal to say about why Turkey should be admitted to the European Union, their opponents on opposition matched them fact for fact.

After the round was over, the two teams engaged in the customary handshake. Allie then dragged her partner to a quiet corner of the hallway to rehash every single moment of the entire round. It was a tournament with closed adjudication. Judges were forbidden from releasing the results of a round under any circumstances. This meant the girls would not officially know if they had won or lost until the end of the day when the two lucky teams advancing to the Grand Final Round were announced.

"I think we did okay – especially considering we were debating grade twelves," said Allie. She was trying to stay upbeat for Octavia's sake, but she was in truth somewhat nervous. "Poppy and Noah qualified for nationals last year. Aram and Jack beat them in the quarter-finals, but they seem to have gotten even better over the summer. They are for sure one of the best teams here. There would be no shame in losing to them." Since it was Octavia's first tournament, she wanted to prepare her gently for the possibility they might lose, even though Allie herself desperately wanted to win.

Allie wanted to affect a calm attitude so Octavia wouldn't realize how pathologically competitive she really was. In reality, Allie secretly kept a tally in her notes of every single gaffe her opponents made during their speeches. Each time someone said "Um," stumbled over their words, mispronounced a name, or got a fact slightly wrong, Allie put a tick in the corner of her notes. This was her way of keeping track of her opponents' weaknesses. Allie tried to keep this habit on the DL because, while very into winning, she was self-reflexive enough to realize that gleefully recording the mistakes of one's competitors came off as a wee bit intense.

"So, what happens now?" asked Octavia.

"They have to tabulate the results first. Whichever two un-defeated teams had the highest combined speaker scores get to debate in front of everyone in the Grand Final. After that round, the winning team gets to take home the Howard Cup." There was a certain lust in Allie's eyes as she mentioned the trophy's name.

"I think we may be undefeated, and you certainly spoke

well." Octavia was optimistic. They had obviously won their first round. She knew the team from Hotchkiss was smart. They talked a lot about the past failures of "constructive engagement," and made lots of questionable assertions likening allowing Turkey into the EU to Europe's appeasement of Hitler during World War II. Octavia was pretty sure, however, that Allie's rebuttal had effectively taken down all of these points with her argument that the youth of Turkey were changing the political landscape, putting it on a path to reform its civil rights record in the coming decades.

After discussing every aspect of the last round five times over, Octavia and Allie finally returned to the Great Hall to wait for the grand finalists to be announced. Allie gritted her teeth and clenched her fists with anxious anticipation. She ran through every word she'd said for the umpteenth time in her head. Had she used enough statistics? Had she used the term "mutually exclusive" too many times? Had she made enough eye contact with that sullen looking judge with the white beard who kind of resembled a grumpy Santa Claus?

Allie looked over at Octavia, who seemed totally at peace, and felt a surge of envy. Why couldn't she be that cool and collected? Why did she have to torture herself about things she could not control? After all, it was not as if worrying about debate rounds once they were over would accomplish anything. Little did Allie know, however, that Octavia was merely pretending to be relaxed. She was just as stressed as Octavia; she was simply more skilled at *pretending* to be calm.

If anything, Octavia was even more worried than her partner, because she knew that a victory today was the only thing that could convince Headmistress Carole that Ms. Knole had done the right thing by disobeying her. Even if they won, there was still a good chance she would be fired. Octavia felt a pang of sadness at the idea of losing Ms. Knole. She was the only adult she'd ever encountered who held her to a high standard, and Octavia was starting to like that.

Jack, like all the other coaches, had been asked to judge rounds. Being a meticulous adjudicator, he spent about fifteen minutes pouring over his notes after every debate before finally deciding who won and the speaker scores each participant deserved. When he did arrive at The Great Hall, the girls had been sitting there ruminating for a while. Part of Jack wanted to avoid Allie all together, but no matter what mistakes had been made, he was still Allie's coach. It was his responsibility to be there for her and Octavia. He approached cautiously, wondering what it would feel like to look Allie in the eye for the first time since The Kiss.

"So how are you feeling?" Jack asked. For a second, Allie froze, thinking he might be referring to the events of the day before.

Octavia was the first to answer. "It was good. I mean, part of me couldn't believe I was actually the nerd who got out of bed early on a Saturday morning to attend the Intellectual Olympics." Here Octavia paused for a second, smiling. "But I liked it. It was fun."

"That's great, Octavia!" He turned to Allie, about to ask for her impressions of the tournament, but her cold expression made him think differently. "Have you seen Lainey and Bailey?"

Allie tersely informed him they were over by the snack table at the back of the room, loading up on mini blueberry muffins. In a flash, Jack was gone. Octavia contemplated why Allie seemed so cool to Jack. She was usually only too happy to banter with him playfully. In fact, if Allie had been anyone else, Octavia would have suspected her of flirting with him, but Allie the rigid rule-follower was definitely not the sort of girl one would suspect of being "hot for the teacher."

After another half hour of waiting, a distinguished looking middle-aged man in a charcoal grey suit approached the microphone. It was Mr. Mansbridge, Jack's father and the Headmaster of Hillsview. The day's results had been tabulated. He was here to announce the teams advancing to the final round.

Allie turned toward Octavia, unexpectedly grabbing her hand. "Octavia, no matter what happens, I want you to know I'm glad you showed up today."

Octavia had never been one for sentimentality, but for some reason this gesture did not seem so mushy. "I'm glad I showed up too, Allie."

Hand in hand, the two young women waited to hear their fate.

16.
WAITING IT OUT

ANNA DECIDED NOT TO wait in The Great Hall for the results with everyone else. Instead, she hid in a nearby science classroom, pacing back and forth, trying to figure out what, exactly, she would do if she lost her job today.

Anna had gone back to ABC to work as a guidance counsellor because she was desperate. Anna loved academia, but she had gotten sidetracked from her research while studying for her PhD at MIT. Ironically, the distraction that had prevented the twenty-five-year-old Fulbright Scholar from tackling her dissertation was none other than her supervisor, Dr. Julian Delacroix.

At first, Anna had been charmed by Dr. Delacroix's insistence that she "call him Julian."

"Please don't see me as your superior, Anna. I am your colleague, your partner if you will. Call me Julian."

Charmed by his booming, deep voice and his dapper floral bowties, Anna was only too happy to think of her supervisor as a friend. It made her feel as though she were finally an adult. Here was a brilliant forty-year-old man who had been published in all the finest psychology journals in the world. He was a genius, and he was treating Anna like an equal. She began to look forward to their weekly meetings like a child looks forward to a play date with her favourite uncle.

Anna knew Julian was a married man with a six-year-old son. Though she was aware that he was ruggedly handsome with adorable dimples and a full head of sandy blonde hair, Anna never really thought of him as anything more than a mentor. This happy collaboration continued until one day Julian himself made it known he saw Anna as more than a student.

It was two years into her PhD when Julian offered to take Anna out for drinks at an off-campus pub to celebrate passing her comprehensive exams. Anna reluctantly agreed to share a bottle of wine with Julian despite not having eaten much that day. After they polished off their first bottle of Malbec, Julian suggested another and, as she was already somewhat uninhibited by tipsiness, Anna agreed.

Halfway into their second bottle of wine, when Julian grabbed her hand under the table, she let him take it reflexively, without thinking. An hour later, when he suggested she come back to his office to sample a forty-year-old Scotch, Anna was too woozy to listen to her instincts. Besides, he was practically dragging her there by the arm.

Once they arrived at in his office, Julian closed the door, and then kissed Anna aggressively. In her drunken haze, Anna didn't exactly have the strength to push him off. She remembered little of what happened after that.

When Anna woke up the next morning somehow back in her apartment, she felt overcome by feelings of horror. She shook with disbelief, and wept for the entire rest of the day. Her world as she knew it was over.

Anna felt desperate. She took to shutting herself into her apartment, subsisting off of various dips and pita bread delivered to her door by Boston Organics. Not even Carlos, who could usually jolly Anna out of any foul mood, was able to lift her spirits. After weeks of playing hooky – something Anna, who was usually a perfect student, had never before done in her life – she accepted defeat.

Ann decided she could not continue her PhD at MIT. She simply couldn't look Julian in the face again. Anna knew she could, in theory, ask for a new supervisor, but she dreaded explaining the reason.

When she was thinking logically, Anna knew enough about the rules of consent to understand she had been taken advantage of by someone in a position of authority who had used alcohol as a means of drugging her. She knew, intellectually, that none of what had happened was her fault. Indeed, if the same events had occurred in the life of a friend or relative, she would have felt nothing but sympathy for her and anger at the offending professor. Still, Anna couldn't face the buildings of MIT. She couldn't face her school friends or the administration. Each time she considered complaining to the administration, she thought, *Who would believe me over him? He's world famous and I'm still a student!*

At the end of the day, MIT was a place full of ghosts and trauma. The worst question, the one that Anna knew was silly and wrong but couldn't help asking herself, however, was this: *Am I partly to blame?* She replayed the night in her mind over and over again. What if she'd only told her supervisor she was too busy to go out with him? What if she'd stopped after the first bottle of wine? What if, what if, what if? It was enough to drive her over the edge, and so she decided to do what her parents referred to as "taking a leave of absence from her doctoral program," but what felt to her like dropping out. She told no one the real reason she couldn't continue, only that she was "too tired," which, in a way, was correct.

Months passed, and soon it was August but Anna still had no life plan. Her mother, who was on the ABC Board of Governors, heard about the guidance counsellor posting and insisted Anna apply.

"You have to do something, Anna!" She shouted at her over the phone. "You cannot just loaf about. If you really are tired and need a break from academia like you say, then fine, but you have to be productive."

"I know, Mom. I just can't work at ABC," Anna replied. She thought of Rajeev Lahiri, and how difficult it would be to spend time with him every day. He might be married with children by now for all she knew. Could she bear seeing him in the hallways?

"Why, Anna?" her mother demanded. "It's as good a job as any and you loved going to that school. Can you think of a good reason not to work there?"

Of course, Anna could indeed think of a good reason working at ABC was not the best idea for her, but she could not tell her mother. She accepted the job, and despite herself, she came to enjoy her work quite quickly. After a few weeks in her new position, Anna felt like she had the potential to make a difference in the lives of students like Allie and Octavia. She was beginning to relish her work.

Anna cursed her luck. How could it be that just as she was beginning to love the job she hadn't even wanted, here she was, pacing in the classroom of an all-boys preparatory school, waiting to be fired?

By the time Rajeev arrived in the doorway looking for her, Anna had completely lost track of time. "Anna, I've been looking everywhere for you!" he said, throwing his hands up in the air in mock frustration.

"Oh, sorry, Rajeev. The pressure is contagious in The Great Hall! I had to step out of that den of adolescent nerves and jut chill for a minute." Anna immediately regretted using the word 'chill.' It sounded disingenuous, as though she was trying too hard to sound natural, which she was.

Rajeev cleared his throat. "Well, the good news is that Allie and Octavia made the final round," he said brightly.

"That's amazing!" Anna was overjoyed for a second, and then a feeling of bitter-sweetness overtook her. Rajeev had yet to tell Anna the bad news. There was a good chance Headmistress Carole had found out that Anna had absconded with Octavia and was already resolved to fire her.

"Just tell me the bad news, Rajeev. Get it over with. I can take it." Anna steeled herself.

"Look, Headmistress Carole called me. She asked if Octavia was here. I said yes and all she said was that she would be right over. She didn't ask how she got here. There's a chance she doesn't know." Rajeev paused. When he spoke again, he sounded more serious. "Anna, if that's true, if she doesn't know, I'll just say I was the one who brought Octavia today." He seemed determined to take the fall.

Anna was touched by Rajeev's offer. Anna was sure that Rajeev still hadn't even paid off his student debt from university, so the fact he was willing to lose his job for her was incredibly heroic. For the first time in her life, however, Anna felt like an honest-to-goodness grown woman. Maybe she was terribly worried and even a little bit petrified, but she did not need anyone to save her.

Anna smiled at Rajeev. "The fact that you would consider doing that for me is incredibly sweet, but I don't need you to bail me out. In fact, I won't LET you do it. I knew the risk I was taking defying my boss. I just didn't agree with her. I thought Octavia deserved a second chance," declared Anna with conviction.

"I love that about you, Anna. You have such a big heart. You always have." Anna said nothing in response, but smiled with her eyes. The pair walked back towards The Great Hall side-by-side, ready to watch their students compete for the Howard Cup with pride.

When it was announced Allie and Octavia had advanced to the final round, Allie was excited but Octavia was euphoric. Here she was, being recognized for something she'd done right. It was a new rush for her, and one that didn't come from sneaking into a bar to have a cocktail. Octavia had spent most of her life avoiding being a goody-goody, as if trying her best at things were somehow selling out, but today she realized how rewarding it could be to work hard.

For her part, Allie's happiness about making the final was somewhat dampened by the task ahead. The team they would be facing was from Phillips Exeter. They had faced Aram and Jack in the semifinal of the National Championships the year before. They were suave and experienced. Allie knew beating the boys would take a Herculean effort.

When Octavia first laid eyes on Basil All-Hussein and Liam Conaway earlier that morning, she leaned over to Allie and asked conspiratorially, "Who are they? Those boys have more swag than a gifting suite at the Grammys."

"Don't stare at them!" hissed Allie in response. "They're the team to beat at this tournament. We can't show any weakness!"

"Oh my God, do you seriously think those Jedi mind tricks are going to make a difference?" Octavia was incredulous.

"Yes, I do. Part of winning is acting worthy of winning. Look, if we have to debate them at some point today, I don't want them thinking we are simpering fans. Debate is a sport where the boys usually dominate and the girls fall at their feet for it. I don't want them to think we hero-worship them just because they have sexy voices that are deeper than the Atlantic Ocean."

Octavia had never heard Allie refer to anything as sexy before. In fact, Octavia once heard Allie refer to a topless picture of Ian Somerhalder as "meh." Octavia was now fairly certain that Allie, whether she herself acknowledged it, was attracted to at least one of the boys on that team.

What Octavia did not know, however, was that almost everyone was attracted to Basil. In addition to being strikingly eloquent, tall, dark, and broodingly handsome, he was also the Crown Prince of Jordan. In short, he was considered the most eligible bachelor on the New England debating circuit. If he'd grown up in a pack of wolves, he would have been the undisputed Alpha Male.

Now, a few hours later, it was time for Allie and Octavia to compete against these high school debate team Alpha males.

Octavia was used to hockey-playing Alpha males who were too woozy from keg stands to say very much, so the concept of dudes who had acquired a legion of devoted fans from expounding on the ideas of Thomas Hobbes' public speeches was somewhat discombobulating. Sure enough, however, all the young women assembled in the audience were twittering in anticipation of hearing the boys speak. Several of them even held up handmade signs on construction paper that read things like, "Go Basil and Liam! You're so hot!"

Allie and Octavia climbed the stairs up to the stage at the front of The Great Hall where the debate would take place. They were on opposition. Much to Allie's consternation, Basil and Liam won the coin toss and decided to take the Government side. Given that Basil had been schooled in Middle Eastern politics since birth in preparation for his future role as King of Jordan, any respectable bookie would have considered Allie and Octavia's chances of winning pretty grim.

Allie was in the middle of a crisis of confidence. This was the very opportunity for which she had been waiting. She desperately wanted to show every debater in the New England area how much she had improved since grade nine. By contrast, Allie felt Octavia had nothing to lose. This was only her first tournament and she had still made final. Even if she just stood there whistling the tune to a One Direction song instead of delivering her speech, no one would have really judged her for it. Octavia's inexperience was her armour.

Allie was attempting to calm herself with more yogic breathing when she noticed a statuesque middle-aged woman in an expertly tailored navy blue suit enter the room. It was Headmistress Carole and she looked furious.

"Octavia, I think Ms. Carole is here. Also, she looks mad. I'm willing to bet Ms. Knole's decision to spring you was not well received?"

Octavia studied the grimace on the elegant middle-aged woman's nearly wrinkle-free face. "No, she does not look happy at all." Octavia began to panic. "Oh God, do you think she'll make me go home right now?"

While a little worried herself, Allie noticed how invested Octavia felt in the round, and it pleased her. "No, I don't think she would cause a scene by interfering with the Grand Final like that. She's not a Real Housewife of New Jersey. I think we're safe, for now."

"Good point. But listen, Allie. This morning, when Ms. Knole came to get me, she said that we had to win or she was pretty sure she'd get fired. At the time I hoped she was being paranoid, but Ms. Carole looks angrier than Bailey when someone doubts the veracity of her gluten allergy." Not wanting to work herself up, Octavia paused for a calming breath. Then added, "Do you think she may have come here to fire Ms. Knole on the spot?"

Allie suddenly understood the gravity of the situation. Winning this debate was no longer just about her individual hopes and dreams. She sat up straighter in her chair. "It's okay, Octavia, we are going to show Headmistress Carole she made the wrong decision." Allie no longer felt nervous, only determined. She sat up straight in her chair and reviewed her notes one final time.

When the debate began a minute later, Basil and Liam still looked as relaxed as ever. They performed their ritual pre-round fist bump. Then they proceeded to give incredibly clear and confident speeches. Their booming deep voices commanded the room, and Basil's charm electrified everyone when he winked at the audience after he finished his Prime Minister's opening address.

Octavia held her own as Member of the Opposition. She talked about the economic ramifications of allowing Turkey into the European Union while Europe is still trying to reverse the damage done during the banking collapse. Allie had been somewhat concerned Octavia might crack under the pressure of her first Grand Final. There were so many people in the audience, and most of them were rooting for the other team.

It was an experience that could have thrown anyone off their game; however, in the end, Octavia's speech was nothing but professional. She knew exactly what she was going to say, forgot not a single fact, and once again wagged her pointer finger to sassy effect.

Eventually, it came time for Allie's address as Leader of the Opposition, the second and final speech for the Opposition side in a round of parliamentary debate. While Octavia's performance was solid, Allie feared her speech would not be enough to earn them a victory.

As Allie walked toward the podium in the centre of the stage, she wondered if she could possibly hold the attention of so many people for ten whole minutes. When they spoke, Basil and Liam's booming voices commanded the attention of everyone in a ten-mile radius. They made a series of jokes the judges seemed to eat up with spoons. For example, Basil had told the room, "Just because the European Union slipped on Greece during the economic collapse, that doesn't mean they don't deserve to enjoy some Turkey. Let's bring on the cranberry sauce!" While Allie herself had cringed at the series of cheesy puns, the crowd seemed to love them. What really elevated his mediocre humour, however, was the fact that Basil seemed to be having fun. He was enjoying himself, and the crowd, seemingly picking up on this, was having a blast as well.

Allie tentatively approached the microphone. Her bravado from before the round started suddenly forgotten. Her stomach was turning and her heart rate felt unnaturally fast. When Allie opened her mouth to speak, for just a moment, she was not sure the words would come. Finally, after an awkwardly long silence, Allie began her speech. "Ladies and gentleman, I will be closing the opposition's case here today. By the end of my speech, there will be no doubt that now is not the appropriate time for the nation-state of Turkey to join the European Union." Allie could feel her palms sweating and she feared her feet would give out. She was tempted to run off stage, out of Hillsview.

She could escape. She could go to a public school where no one knew her and where the budget cuts were so severe they could not afford a debate team at all. While the social justice warrior in Allie knew it was horribly unfair how many fewer opportunities students at public schools often received, at that moment, the idea of attending an under-funded institution seemed more than a little appealing to her.

Allie, thirty seconds into her speaking time, was in the middle of what was becoming a second awkwardly long pause when she suddenly caught site of Ms. Knole sitting in the front row. Allie looked into the kind eyes of the woman who risked her job to help her and Octavia. How could she let her down? Allie knew she held Ms. Knole's job in her hands. She knew that if she couldn't get it together, it would all be over. The pressure was, of course, intense, and yet, Allie simultaneously felt inspired. Anna Knole had bet on her and Octavia as a team. She risked everything for them because she thought they were capable. If someone could have that much faith in her, Allie knew it was her duty to try her absolute hardest to believe in herself.

Allie took a deep breath. With a renewed sense of purpose, she remembered her mission. This time, she had no plans to forget that determination.

"Ladies and gentleman, my constructive argument is about the problems with letting Turkey into the European Union in light of its current government's poor human rights record." Allie took a deep breath. She knew what she had to do. It would be a risk, but if she didn't take it, they would certainly lose. Allie continued, "One could even say, that Turkey is a lot like Little Miss Muffet.... It has Kurds in its way." The audience erupted in laughter. The reaction was beyond Allie's wildest dreams. While the audience had laughed good-naturedly and her opponent's jokes, the spectators were now doubled over in fits of laughter in response to Allie. Many spectators even clapped, they found her comment so witty.

Allie smiled at the room. So this is what it was like to have an audience in the palm of one's hand! "In all seriousness," she continued. "Turkey's current human rights stance on the Kurdish people is particularly troubling," before inundating the room with well-researched facts, such as the government's history of jailing Kurds – even children – at peaceful protests.

When Allie returned to her seat, Octavia leaned over to whisper, "See! I told you they would like the Little Miss Muffet joke!" As much as Allie had originally doubted her, she admitted Octavia had been right all along.

As was the custom, after The Grand Final of the Howard Cup was complete, the five judges retired to the headmaster's office nearby to choose the victors. The audience itself was divided regarding who won, with the young men and women who had soft spots for tall, dark and handsome princes siding with Basil's team.

Meanwhile, Allie and Octavia were too distracted by panicking over whether Ms. Knole was about to lose her job to spend much time wondering if they had won or lost the round. Both girls watched Headmistress Carole like a hawk. Fortunately, Headmaster Mansbridge had spotted her as soon as the round was over and engaged her in a chat about planning for the upcoming holiday bazaar the two schools co-hosted together.

"Wow, Jack's dad is really chatty," remarked Octavia to Allie.

"At least it buys us some time," Allie responded. Though she was not sure what, exactly, they could do with it.

Allie and Octavia's conversation was soon interrupted by none other than Anna herself approaching. She was beaming at them. She looked proud, not at all fearful.

"You girls were AMAZING!" Anna shrieked in enthusiastic tones. "I just want you both to know that no matter what happens, I am so extremely proud of both of you." She looked Octavia in the eyes. "You were phenomenal! Who could believe you only started this year?" She turned to Allie next. "And you, Miss! You are a superstar. Where have you been hiding that killer sense of humour?" But before Allie or Octavia could reply, they heard a voice echoing from a microphone informing everyone to return to their seats, the results of the Howard Cup were ready.

When Allie and Octavia heard their names called out as the winners of the Howard Cup, Octavia's heart skipped a beat. Meanwhile, Allie who had longed for this moment for such a long time, was convinced she was dreaming. Octavia had to pull her up out of her seat and practically drag her back up on stage to receive their trophy from Mr. Mansbridge.

In no time, the girls were besieged by a sea of admirers congratulating them on their performance. One particularly nervy grade nine from Roxbury Latin School even slipped Octavia his phone number on a scrap of paper under the guise of "shaking her hand." Anna and Rajeev had to herd the girls through the sea of fans so they wouldn't be crushed.

When the full ABC complement finally exited the building, however, reality sunk in. There were no more groupies, and Headmistress Carole was standing there waiting for them. Everyone knew to whom she intended to speak.

At first, the girls thought they might rally around Ms. Knole, but Headmistress Carole made short work of that plan by waiting patiently for the girls' parents to collect them before making a move. Allie had wanted to stay to protect Ms. Knole, but Sybilla was insistent about leaving in time to make her squash game. There was no time to explain the gravity of the situation to her mother, so Allie grudgingly got in the SUV.

Soon, Octavia was the only one left, as she had no parents in Boston to speak of. Seizing the moment, Ms. Carole said evenly, "Mr. Lahiri, could you please take Octavia inside for a moment?" Rajeev reluctantly obliged. For a moment, he considered acting on his plan to take the fall himself, but he knew Anna would never allow it.

When everyone was out of earshot. Headmistress Carole put on the disappointed face she had perfected after years of catching teenagers trying to sneak cans of beer into their senior proms. "Anna, I have known you since you were twelve years old."

Anna nodded, remembering how much she had always respected Ms. Carole when she was a child. She had never gotten in trouble with the headmistress when she was a student at ABC, but now, after only a matter of weeks as a guidance counsellor, she had managed to commit what was almost definitely an unforgiveable offense.

"I never thought you were the type to defy me so flagrantly. And while it is lovely that ABC won the Howard Cup today for the first time in years, that doesn't change the fact it was most unprofessional of you to go behind my back and against my wishes."

Anna could not believe how stoic Headmistress Carole was. She was a woman of steel. Anna began to wonder how she could have been so naïve as to have ever thought that if the girls only won the tournament, Ms. Carole might forgive everything. Anna braced herself to lose her job. She wondered what she would tell her parents, who already judged her so harshly for abandoning her PhD. Now they would think she was a complete failure!

Ms. Carole cleared her throat in an ominous way. "So, I want you to know that I am both shocked and disappointed by your actions. Please do not undermine me like that again in your work with our girls."

Anna reeled. Could it be possible she was getting a second chance? "Ms. Carole, please forgive my confusion. Does this mean I still have a position at ABC? I thought you were going to ... well, fire me...."

"Don't be so dramatic. Leave that to the teenage students." Ms. Carole flashed what almost looked like a smile. "Well, I'd best be off. I have to attend a fundraiser for Elizabeth Warren tonight." With that, she turned and headed towards her black Volvo at the other side of the parking lot.

Meanwhile a shocked Anna was left digesting the fact she was still gainfully employed.

Rajeev and Anna escorted Octavia back to ABC in Anna's car. Exhausted from the day, hardly anyone spoke during the ten-minute drive. They sat in the satisfied silence that is the reward of a job well done.

After they arrived back at ABC and Octavia had safely entered the boarding house, Rajeev turned to Anna. He looked at her with his soulful eyes for several seconds, then asked meaningfully, "So, what are you doing this evening?"

"I don't know, catching up on those episodes of *Scandal* waiting for me on my DVR? I guess I'm not too exciting," Anna laughed.

"Oh, I disagree," replied Rajeev. "You are the most exciting person I know."

Anna felt flustered. She looked down at the ground nervously, afraid of what she would reveal if she made eye contact with Rajeev at that moment.

"Anna, you did a great thing today. You really helped two kids and you risked your own interests to do so. You amaze me." He paused for a deep breath, Rajeev's voice became softer as he added, "It made me wonder why I ever let you go."

"Rajeev, let's not think about that. It was so long ago. There's no point. You're with Melissa now."

But Rajeev couldn't drop the subject. He ventured, "What happened? Why did you end it? Didn't you love me back?"

"I loved you so much! How can you question that?" Anna felt hurt. "I broke up with you because I loved you. No one would have believed us that we just happened to meet by fluke at a bookstore in Cambridge the night after my graduation." Anna paused, remembering how she had left her prom to attend a Jon Stewart book signing. She arrived in her floor-length pink prom dress with every intention of getting his autograph, then returning to the party before anyone noticed she was gone. Anna never expected to find Rajeev in the crowd, to start a conversation with him, to spend the rest of the night talking with him until four a.m. She had not expected to fall in love, but how many people ever do?

Anna was now blinking back tears remembering how difficult it had been to end things with Rajeev. She had made the decision one day after they narrowly avoided being seen by an ABC parent on a daytrip to the Cape. Rajeev hadn't seemed rattled by it, but Anna knew if they had been caught, the whole world would know about the two of them in under five minutes.

Anna pleaded, "Rajeev, you know I'm right. No one would have believed that we weren't involved with each other when you were a student teacher at ABC." Anna grew more and more frantic. "You would have lost all of your professional credibility, Rajeev. And ABC NEVER would have hired you on permanently. No one would have."

"Well, in the end I lost you. Do you think that was better?" Rajeev sounded frustrated, angry, and sad, all at the same time.

"The thought of you destroying your career before it even began was something I couldn't stomach. I wanted you, but I didn't want to ruin your reputation and your career in order to have you. I thought it would be selfish to let you give up everything else you had worked for just for me." Anna paused to wipe tears from her eyes. "The guilt was too much for an eighteen-year-old girl to bear."

Rajeev sighed. "I may wish you had seen things differently seven years ago, but maybe things can be different now." He paused, mustering the courage to ask the question that had been on the tip of his tongue since seeing Anna Knole again a few weeks before. "Why did you come back, Anna? I know you must have moved on. I know you have so much going for you, but of all the schools in the world, why did you come back to ABC?" Rajeev hoped he was at least a small part of the reason.

In that moment, Anna wished things were simpler. She wished should could say she had sought out the job at ABC to be near Rajeev. It would have seemed stalkerish and obsessive, but it was easier to explain than the truth.

Anna wanted Rajeev. These past few weeks at ABC had made her realize she had never loved anyone else as much, and yet part of her was afraid of telling him what she had gone through at MIT. What if he didn't believe her professor's advances were unwanted? What if he blamed her for the whole thing, like the tiny voice inside her head, which try as she might, she could not completely silence?

Instead of telling him the truth, she decided to tell Rajeev a different story. While none of it was true, at least Anna knew how he would react to it.

Anna ventured, "Rajeev, I had no choice. I had to drop out of my PhD eight weeks ago because I had an inappropriate relationship with my professor. I instigated it. He was married and had a child. The whole lot. What can I say? I guess I've always had a thing for my teachers." Rajeev recoiled. He was clearly hurt by the idea that their love affair was part of a seedy pattern.

Anna continued her fabrication: "Eventually, the sneaking around got old, you know? So I ended it with my prof. When it was over, I felt like I couldn't continue working with him. I needed something else to do and being the guidance counsellor at ABC was the only job offer I had. My mom's still on the board of governors, so I used her connections." As she finished her speech, the pained expression on Rajeev's face made Anna want to disappear forever.

"Oh ... I see," Rajeev said gravely. He was attempting to affect a casual tone and failing miserably at it.

Anna wished she could have trusted Rajeev with the truth. She was fairly certain he would believe her. If she'd felt up to taking that risk, perhaps they could even have ended up together? Anna knew there was a possibility she could have had everything she'd ever wanted, but the words she needed to share the truth just wouldn't come.

But then, as they stood there in silence, Anna's mind wandered. Anna thought back to high school. Rajeev was the student teacher who'd lectured girls in the hall if he heard them use the word "slut." Surely someone so enlightened wouldn't blame her for what happened that night? Suddenly, Anna felt more confident. If he only knew her real story, Rajeev would most likely understand. She frantically began to backtrack, regretting everything she had said out of fear. "Rajeev, it's not what you think. I ... misspoke? Please, allow me to explain," Anna pleaded.

"You don't have to explain anything to me, Anna." Rajeev paused, before adding, "Look I have to go. I'm supposed to go to a dinner party with Melissa tonight."

Rajeev began to exit the car before Anna could plead with him to listen. Before he closed the car door, however, he called to Anna, "I'll see you on Monday, okay?" Suddenly, Rajeev sounded like his old jovial self, even though both he and Anna knew it was all an act.

Rajeev walked away not judging Anna for having been with a married man. He didn't know all the circumstances, and besides, it was the guy in question who was breaking his commitment. He did, however, walk away less certain that what he and Anna had was as special to her as it was to him. Maybe, what she'd said had been true. Maybe she really did just have "a thing" for her teachers. Rajeev felt like a fool for having spent so long believing Anna was the love of his life. She was his colleague, and that was all he could afford to see her as from now on.

When Anna and Rajeev escorted Octavia back to Hillsview, Octavia spied someone very unexpected in the parking lot:

Bailey's boyfriend Austin. Craftily, she pretended to go inside the boarding house. Then she snuck right back out after she saw Anna and Rajeev fully engrossed in conversation with one another from the window. She was confident they were so absorbed with one another they would never notice her outside loitering freely. "Hey there, Austin!" she said with a shy smile. Octavia wasn't used to feeling shy, but Austin brought that feeling out in her. "What are you doing here?"

"I'm picking my little sister up from play practice. She's in grade nine. She's in the chorus of *Annie*."

"That's really nice of you!" The old Octavia wasn't so impressed by niceness, but this one could admit it was cool Austin cared for his sister.

"So, I hear from Bailey that you won the debate at Hillsview today. Congratulations! I'm a terrible public speaker myself, so I have a lot of respect for your ability. I always bomb my class presentations." Austin's blue eyes shone in the late-afternoon light. It was unclear how anyone could be so handsome.

"Maybe I could help you prepare for a presentation sometime?" Octavia ventured without thinking. She knew Austin was technically taken. It would not be advantageous for Octavia if the invitation got back to Bailey, but the offer was out there now.

Much to her surprise, however, Austin seemed delighted. "I would love that!" Just as the words came out of his mouth, a cute fourteen-year-old bounded out the doors of ABC. It was Austin's sister Izzie. She was full of energy and clearly had no idea she was ruining a "moment."

"Okay, I'm ready to go home! Let's hit the road, Ozzie!"

Austin blushed. "That's my nick name." He began fumbling with the keys to the family SUV to play for time. "I'll see you around, Octavia?"

"I'll see you around, Austin."

As she watched Austin and Izzie drive off, Octavia felt a sense of excitement. She wasn't sure what was to come, but she had to admit after the day's events, ABC was starting to feel more like home.

Jack had barely gotten to speak to Allie since The Kiss. At the Howard Cup, she had more or less ignored him. After her victory with Octavia, Allie was so surrounded by well-wishers, Jack was barely able to congratulate her at all.

Jack had never seen Allie have more fun in her life than he had in The Grand Final round of the Howard Cup that afternoon. Allie Denning had let loose. She was so self-possessed and articulate. By now, Jack was used to feeling attracted to Allie, but now he realized how much she had come into herself. Allie did not just look like a grown woman, she was starting to act like one too.

Jack began to question Aram's threats to stay away from his little sister, because, frankly, Allie did not seem so little anymore.

As Jack drove back from the Howard Cup to his dorm at Harvard, all he could think of was kissing Allie again. He bitterly regretted rebuffing her advances the night before. After all, who was he to tell her what to do or how to feel? If they both wanted each other, Jack suddenly felt certain that couldn't be so wrong for them to be together.

Jack decided to stop for an espresso at Starbucks, hoping a caffeine boost would help him think more clearly. But all he could think about the whole time was how Allie adored their iced passion-tea lemonades. Out of nowhere, everything was reminding him of her.

The Fun song "We Are Young" was playing in the coffee shop, and it reminded Jack of the time he, Aram, and Allie went to their outdoor concert that summer in Cape Cod. He noticed a girl with a ponytail, Allie's hairstyle of choice, and that too reminded Jack of her. No matter where he turned, Jack could not seem to escape that girl, so he downed his coffee and got back into the car.

Jack knew Allie was at home alone from reading her Facebook status in his newsfeed. It read: "Parents out at Planned Parenthood benefit, home alone with Whole Foods panini and the final season of *The Newsroom* for company. How I love you, Jeff Daniels!"

Jack didn't bother texting Allie before driving over. What he wanted to say, he needed to say in person. That was one thing of which Jack was certain.

Jack rang the doorbell to the Denning House, half-worried Charles and Sybilla might have arrived home earlier than expected. That would put a bit of a wrench in his romantic announcement.

When Allie finally answered the door, she was wearing flannel pajamas with cupcakes on them. She looked a mixture of surprised and annoyed to find Jack there.

"Oh, Jack, hi. What brings you here?" she asked in a tone that could only be described as polite.

"I was wrong."

"Wrong about what?"

"I liked it when you kissed me. I was just afraid because I know Aram wouldn't like it. I convinced myself it was inappropriate to go after my best friend's baby sister, but Allie, you're not a baby anymore. You are an impressive young woman. You blew my mind today. So who am I to say that someone that smart can't make her own decisions about which guys to kiss?" Jack smiled his megawatt smile, the one that usually made girls all over Massachusetts melt.

Allie frowned. "Jack, please stop this. You should go. It's unseemly for you to be at my house at night."

"Unseemly?" Jack repeated in confusion. What on earth was she getting at?

"Listen, you were right. I was wrong to kiss you yesterday, but not because I'm your best friend's little sister. I was wrong because now you're my teacher," said Allie definitively. "Look, winning that debate today felt wonderful. It made me want even more success. I think that you were right, Octavia and I make a great team." Allie paused. "I'm so grateful to you for finding me such an amazing new debate partner. However, Jack, if Octavia and I are going to win nationals someday, I need you to be my coach, not my boyfriend."

Jack was silent.

"If it makes you feel any better, I promise not to tell Aram about any of this. The kiss won't affect your friendship because he'll never know about it. We can forget this ever happened."

Jack knew he couldn't forget the feel of Allie's lips on his, but fairly certain he had no choice but to try, Jack agreed. The kiss had ruined their friendship, and now that Allie had vetoed a romance, their professional relationship was all they had.

Jack did consider pleading his case. He considered promising he could be her coach and her boyfriend, or even offering to quit, but his pride was too wounded to try. Defeated, Jack returned to his car and drove back to Harvard, disappointed and alone.

After Jack left, Allie's heart raced for several long minutes. She felt slightly unsure of her decision. Allie couldn't deny that she still liked him. Ending her feelings for Jack was not as simple as turning off the ringer on your phone when you needed some peace and quiet. Still, Allie felt proud of herself for being strong. She had resisted temptation.

Around eleven p.m., after indulging in five straight episodes of Aaron Sorkin's scripted television, Allie decided to retire to her bed in order to read *The Handmaid's Tale* for an hour before going to sleep. It seemed time to finally read one of her mother's books.

However, Allie had barely started the first chapter when she heard her phone emit a Facebook notification. Initially, she thought it might be Jack, writing to ask her to reconsider their relationship, but instead it was a message from someone very surprising. So surprising, in fact, that Allie didn't believe it at first.

From Basil Al-Hussein:

Hey Allie,

You were brilliant today. I must say, I usually really dislike when I lose, but losing to you was most enjoyable. You have a very advanced understanding of International Relations. How about we discuss the Arab-Israeli conflict sometime over coffee?
Basil

Allie was not sure what to make of this improbable overture from a future Jordanian monarch. She knew every girl in New England would have killed to receive any kind of attention from Basil Al-Hussein, one of the best-looking young men north of California. Allie herself was flattered and excited at the prospect of maybe getting to know him better, but instead of replying right away, she turned off her phone.

"I'll message him tomorrow," Allie said to herself. "I've done enough thinking about boys for one night." With that, she once again picked up her copy of *The Handmaid's Tale,* and began to read.

ACKNOWLEDGEMENTS

This book would not be possible without the support of my partner, family, and friends – thank you.

I would also like to thank our publisher, Inanna Publications, for believing in this manuscript, and trusting us with their first foray into Young Adult for budding feminists.

Last, thank you to my brilliant writing partner Sarah – we did it!

—*Shalta Dicaire Fardin*

I have long said that it takes a village to write a book. Well, not only did I have a fabulous co-author in the form of Shalta, but I would like to thank all the other people, without whom, this book would not have been possible. Having the idea for a novel is one thing, but without the support and enthusiasm of Inanna Publications, as well as all my friends and family, I doubt I would have had the strength to continue with this project.

Firstly, I would like to thank my parents, for sending me to an all-girls school with an excellent debate program. Without that experience, it would never have occurred to me to suggest we write a book about high school debaters at an all-girls school in Boston.

I would like to thank Ingrid, Dianna, Melissa and Joanna, the first people I ever told about the concept for *Good Girls*, way back when I had no idea how we would even start writing it. Robert Embree is another person who deserves a special shout out for being a supportive player in this process. I would like to thank Jen McNeely, for introducing me to publishers and always going above and beyond to help other women realize their dreams. I would also be remiss if I did not thank Kaley Ames, who was the first person to read the manuscript besides me and Shalta. Kaley gave the gentle, encouraging feedback we needed to complete our last draft.

Next, I would like to thank my former student, Sonia Mahajan, who became our first teen reader. Her perspective enriched this project immeasurably. In addition, I must give a special thank you to my student Anna Lisa, for noticing an important typo I overlooked in our proofs. Her sharp eye saved me much anguish.

Of course, we owe the visionary, hardworking and brilliant feminists at Inanna our everlasting gratitude. When I first emailed Renée Knapp, asking about the submission process, I was terrified our book wouldn't meet Inanna Publication's standards. Renée, however, was a bastion of kindness. Without her encouragement, I doubt we would have worked up the gumption to submit our manuscript for consideration. And, obviously, we would be nowhere without the inspirational force of nature that is Luciana Ricciutelli. Luciana, your deft hand as editor has brought out the best in our beloved little book. But my respect for you goes far beyond your skill as an editor. I stand in awe of the feminist press you have built. Your grace, humour, and commitment to feminist writers are gifts to Canadian literature, and to the future of feminist literature everywhere. Thank you for believing in this book.

Finally, I would like to thank all my students. You ground me, humble me, make me laugh, and make me proud. Everything I do, I do with the hope of making the world a slightly better and brighter place for you. Teaching you has been the greatest honour of my adulthood. I learn from your curiosity, your diligence and your passion. You teach me to do better, to be better, and to dream of better things for the world. Like almost everything I do, I wrote this book for you. My dear students, I hope one day we will live in a world that deserves you....

—*Sarah Sahagian*

From left to right, Sarah Sahagian and Shalta Dicaire Fardin.

Shalta Dicaire Fardin has a degree in Gender Studies from Queen's University; her area of academic focus was primarily in constructing identity through physical presentation. Shalta works in the field of advertising and technology, and is passionate about promoting women in STEM fields. She lives in Toronto, Ontario, and for her four-legged child Jasper.

Sarah Sahagian is a PhD Candidate in Gender, Feminist and Women's Studies at York University in Toronto. In her academic writing career, she is the co-editor of *Mother of Invention: How Our Mothers Influenced Us as Academics and Activists* (2013) and *The Mother-Blame Game* (2015). During her time off from academia, Sarah is a regular contributor to the award-winning feminist blog Gender Focus, writing feminist critiques of popular culture and meditations on various feminist issues of the day. She moonlights as a comedy writer for the Canadian satirical news magazine, *The Beaverton*. *Good Girls* is her first novel. She lives in Toronto.